STREET RAISED
PEARCE HANSEN

1

Praise for PEARCE HANSEN & STREET RAISED:

"Street Raised is a scar of a book, but it is a beautifully healed scar. Gutsy, fast-paced, written in an electric style. Recommended."
—Joe Lansdale, author of *The Bottoms* and the *Hap & Leonard* series

"Imagine James Ellroy coupled with George R. R. Martin and overseen by Charles Willeford."
—Ken Bruen, author of the *Jack Taylor* series

"Hansen's delivery is nothing like Cormac McCarthy's, but this novel possessed visceral and nasty surprises that put it in the same territory of viciousness and macabre grandeur as Blood Meridian. There is something of Michael Shea's street beat poetics in Hansen's rhythmic prose, and even a slight hint of what it would look like if Wambaugh stopped giving a rat's ass about anyone else in the entire world, hitched up his suspenders, spit into his cupped palms, and then grabbed an axe and started in with blood in his eye."
—Laird Barron, author of *Occultation* and *The Beautiful Thing That Awaits Us All*.

"In its best passages, Street Raised suggests a contemporary version of Jack Black's classic 1926 memoir of itinerant criminal life, *You Can't Win*—albeit a heavily armed, hyperviolent update."
—Eddie Muller, host of Turner Classic Movies' *Noir Alley* and founder of the Film Noir Foundation.

Cover art and design copyright © 2013 by Matthew Revert
www.matthewrevert.com

Interior design by J David Osborne

Published by Broken River Books in 2013. Published by Point Blank/Wildside Press 2006. Portions of this novel were originally published as short stories in *Mysterical-e,* Anthony Neil Smith's *Plots with Guns!* and Dave Zeltserman's *Hardluck Stories.*

STREET RAISED
PEARCE HANSEN

ACKNOWLEDGEMENTS:

Thank you, James Frey; Jess Mowry and Andrew Vachss. Special thanks always to Allan Guthrie; Anthony Neil Smith; Les Edgerton and Joe Clifford.

This book is dedicated to two absent friends: Pete Peterson and Beau Bixler.

Table of Contents

1: THE STEP-OFF

The Coupe de Ville came upon a river, with a tall steel girder bridge spanning the deep chasm. The tires' whine took on hollow overtones as the car started across the span. Esteban stopped in the middle of the bridge.

Beau climbed out, his sharkskin suit shimmering. Esteban followed suit.

The road spooled away in both directions, an asphalt ribbon glowing dull gray in the moonlight and disappearing into pine-crowded mountains behind and ahead of them.

Beau grasped the back of Esteban's neck with his ring bedizened hand and steered him to the railing. The two brothers stared into the abyss.

Esteban trembled at the long drop. The river sighed past, way too far below, its swirls and ripples sparkling and cold as the water surged past the bridge's inadequate supports.

Beau said, "We're all on a bridge between life and death, hermanito. And this is where these putos step off."

Beau squeezed the back of Esteban's neck and let go. "Oso," Beau said with a directorial gesture of his hand. "Vamanos."

Oso clambered out of the car; his face impassive as he donned his 20-gallon cowboy hat. He reached into the backseat and dragged out the man on top by his bound ankles, the wrapped chains dragging across each other, clanking and clinking in a skirling whir.

When the back of the man's head slipped off the running board, it slammed onto the asphalt with a hollow thud. His eyes blinked and rolled as Oso dragged him to the railing.

Esteban reached into the darkness of the backseat. He hooked his hands into the slackened chains around the other's ankles and started pulling. When the vato was all the way out, Esteban stopped, grabbed his head, and lowered it to the pavement. He flicked a guilty glance at his brother and Oso but they hovered over the man at the railing, muttering to each other as they studied him with pleased expressions on their faces.

Esteban looked down at this vato's head, still cradled in his hands. They made eye contact. A message poured out the vato's eyes, as if he were trying to taint Esteban's soul. Esteban's heart pounded as he wrenched his gaze away from the vato's witchery.

Esteban's right hand crooked in defense against black magic, pinkie and forefinger extended. Avoiding the vato's gaze, Esteban grabbed him by the shoulders and dragged him the rest of the way to the railing, taking care to keep his head off the pavement. Esteban set the vato down next to his partner and stepped back to stand with Beau and Oso.

The other man was blond, still blinking with unfocused eyes – bouncing the back of his head on the road had knocked something loose. The vato was all too conscious of his predicament – a sheen of sweat covered his face, and the whites of his eyes glistened as he stared up at heaven. Esteban hoped that if he was praying, that it was for his immortal soul rather than a miracle.

"So you maricons figured you'd take me off?" Beau asked. "Here comes all the oro you're gonna get from me."

Beau started pissing on the two men. He swept his hips from side to side, the stream of urine arcing out to splash the lengths of their chained bodies and across their faces.

The huero did not react to being pissed on at all, but the vato grunted and shut his eyes tight as he jerked his head to the side. The urine spilled across his cheeks and up his nostrils, prompting a round of sneezing. The vato was still sneezing the piss out his nose when Beau stopped urinating, tucked himself back inside his fly and zipped up.

Oso squatted next to the huero and grabbed two handfuls of chain. He looked up at Esteban with a good-natured grin. "Time to lose your cherry, 'Steban."

Esteban squatted opposite Oso and copied him. With a heave and a grunt the two stood, the chains on the huero clanking as they leaned him against the railing. The huero's face was inches from Esteban's, and his eyes were rolling around, their lids fluttering.

Oso squatted by the huero's ankles, keeping one hand on the chains around the man's waist to hold him erect. Esteban hurried to follow suit.

"Ready?" Oso asked with eyes atwinkle. "Go."

They both stood, heaving the huero's ankles overhead as he endo-ed over the railing. Esteban turned away. Oso looked over the edge the entire time it took for the huero to hit the river with a distant booming splash that elicited a triumphant grunt.

Oso leaned over the vato so their faces were close together.

"Your turn, mamon," Oso said in a bass singsong. A falsetto titter leaked from him.

Esteban squatted next to the vato opposite Oso and they heaved him upright against the rail.

The vato screamed repeatedly, whatever words he was wailing muffled behind the duct-tape. He swung his head from side to side in a frenzy, his ponytail whipping round to spank Oso's face, knocking the killer's cowboy hat awry. Oso flinched away and growled.

The vato shimmied inside his chains, the links clinked and slithered together as he thrashed and gyrated. Esteban and Oso struggled to keep their grips, but Esteban lost hold of the slippery chains and the vato slammed to his side on the pavement. The vato's muffled screaming stopped as he lay stunned.

Beau sneered. "You're blowing it, ese."

Esteban could not look at him or Oso. "It's different, man. This one's all awake and such. It's not like with the blanco."

Beau cocked his head at an angle. "Awake, out cold, what's it to you? Okay, awake is always better – but don't wuss out on me hermanito."

Esteban squatted next to the vato again and glanced at his face, hoping hitting the road like that had knocked him out like his friend. The vato's eyes were tearful as he stared back with a silent plea, and Esteban aimed his gaze away.

They hoisted the man up to the rail once more. The vato shook with a bone-deep trembling as Esteban and Oso stooped by his ankles. It felt like leaking electricity.

"Ready?" Oso asked. "Go."

Esteban ignored Oso, staring into space with a horrified expression on his face. He was as much a prisoner as this poor payaso. "No," he whispered.

"Goddammit lift Esteban you pussy," Beau said.

Snapping out of his trance to obey without thinking, the puppet stood with Oso, heaved up on the vato's feet and let go. He watched as the chain-bound figure toppled end-over-end in slow motion.

The moonlight beamed onto the figure's face for an instant. Esteban saw, not the vato's features, but his own face peering back at him –

The vato hit the river and was gone. Esteban thrust himself away from the rail.

When he next went to Mass, would his hands shake when he lit his candle for granmama? When he told Padre Trejo of this night's work at Confession, how many Hail Marys would he be assigned? How many Acts of Contrition? What Act of Atonement could remove the mortal stain he had just voluntarily put on his own soul?

"Get your ass in gear, 'Steban," Beau said, behind him.

Oso was folded up in the back of the Coupe de Ville like an idling praying mantis. Beau stood by the open passenger door, bored and sulky.

If Esteban stepped far enough out of line, would Beau wrap him in chains and drive him to the river? He knew the answer to that one clear as day.

Esteban walked around to the driver's side, his mind spinning. He opened the door but then stood there as he realized with a panicked thrill that Beau was just another meat bag too – born to die like everybody else.

"You getting in or what?" his big brother asked from the

darkness inside the car.

Esteban wrestled his face toward blankness as his mind scampered away to less dangerous ideas. By the time he slid into the driver's seat he displayed no emotion at all.

2: GUN PUNK

Willy moved through white blankness between islands of light surrounding the haloed streetlamps. A skinny freckle faced kid with tangled shoulder length red hair, wearing a Pendleton, frayed-cuffed flood bell bottoms and raggedy Adidas trainers.

He was in the Bushrod Park district of North Oakland. Buoys clanged out on the Bay, echoing across the water. The Marina South Light foghorn sounded to the northwest. Willy could faintly hear the two horns on Alcatraz Island, sounding the opening bars to some beautiful piece of music which never materialized.

Houses loomed stark out of the fog as he approached them, only to dissolve as he passed. His face was strange and he was in fugue state – he would have been unwilling or unable to speak if anyone had approached him right now, but he was alone and safe in the clean sea-smelling fog. As he walked, he sensed the world squirming around him: a planet full of drones and puppets stumbling through unexamined lives – and him an alien spy among them.

He reached a double-decker hot sheet motel and studied it, steeling and hardening himself back from egoless-ness. The stucco exterior of the motel was swathed with cryptic West Side graffiti tags, and bled condensation from the fog.

Willy moved around back in a stroll. He reached the rear of the motel and looked up at the door to Room 222 on the second floor, at the top of the exterior staircase. He rotated 360 degrees in place. He stopped to face 222, closing his eyes: nothing but the fog-muffled sound of distant invisible traffic.

He ascended the exterior staircase, treading with care. He

extended the palm of one hand to hover an inch away from the scarred gray door. He leaned toward the door, inclining his head without quite touching his ear to its surface. He heard Johnny Carson make a snide comment on the TV inside, followed by Ed McMahon's chortle.

Willy took a black woolen ski mask from his back pocket and tugged it over his face. He darted glances at the neighboring motel rooms and at the parking lot over his shoulder. He drew his .45 from under his Pendleton and knocked on the door.

He heard Sherri's voice from inside say, "Let's see who it is," countered by her john saying, "Fuck that noise."

The bolt was thrown. Little Willy slammed the motel door open and snaked to the center of the room in a lunge, his .45 springing up to aim at the two occupants.

Sherri, a chicken-breasted crack whore, stumbled back from Willy's threat and cringed next to her john: a bald skinny man of about sixty with workman's hands, wearing a mechanic's jacket with 'Sonny' embroidered over the heart. He held a motel glass with whiskey slopping out to spill as he glared at Willy.

"It's not even a good fake," Sonny said, scowling bushy-browed at the quite real .45.

The old man lumbered toward Willy making a grab for his hardware, and Willy took a step back. Willy's back slammed against the door as he took one more step away from Sonny's swipes.

Willy prodded the geezer in the chest with the muzzle of the .45. Sonny gasped, clapped one hand against his chest and his eyes rolled up in his head as he sank to the carpet.

"Predicate, special circumstances," Little Willy muttered, goggling down at the dead mark. "Life without for homicide in the commission."

Willy pressed two fingers against the side of the old man's throat. Sonny's heart beat strongly.

Sherri leaned toward him as he pocketed Sonny's bankroll. "Willy," she said. "Little Willy's the man."

She was still whispering his name as he whirled away from her and the mark, who squirmed in a backstroke on the floor as he approached consciousness.

Willy booked out the door and down the staircase, two at a time. The hollow concrete-over-steel steps boomed beneath his feet like Caribbean drums. At the foot of the stairs he doubled over, clutching at his head with an expression of sudden agony. He recovered and vaulted the waist-high wall at the rear of the lot into the alley beyond.

There was a smash cut in his memory and the next thing he knew he was in the hotel hallway outside Marla's third floor room with no time lapse he could recall. He knocked on the door, Marla opened, and Little Willy crowded past her into the room.

The stench of crack smoke filled the air.

Marla's pedal pushers hung loose on spindly legs, her face bony, her nails chewed to the quick.

Ghost sat in the easy chair: a tall angular man with his hoodie cinched tight around his sketch of a face.

A jheri-curled older Black man occupied the sofa, wearing an orange leather jacket and horn-rim glasses held together by masking tape at the bridge.

"Sherman," Willy said. Sherman settled his taped glasses on his nose with his middle finger.

Little Willy counted his bankroll. The other three watched the green intently. Willy handed two C-notes to Ghost and the rest to Sherman.

Sherman took two huge cocaine rocks from his pocket, which he handed to Willy. Sherman stood and listened at the door, then cracked it open and listened again before pulling a bamboo flute from his jacket. He stepped into the hallway, put the flute sideways to his mouth and began playing a soft, atonal series of notes.

The music sounded all Japanese-y to Willy, like sake and samurais and such-like. Sherman's flute song grew quieter as he Kwai-Chang-Cain-ed off down the hall. Quieter still when Marla closed the door.

Marla handed Willy a straight-shooter pipe and produced a butane torch which she lit and held for him. He heated the pipe then placed a rock on the end to melt into the chunk of copper cleaning pad stuck there as a screen. Marla held the torch as he took a cook hit. He jerked the pipe away from the torch as white filled the tube and a tendril of smoke wavered from the end to dissipate. Marla held the torch to the rock and he sucked hard as white smoke billowed till he could inhale no more.

Willy sank back against the couch cushions, holding this lungful of smoke with every bit of concentration he could muster. Marla plucked the pipe from Willy's hand as the rush overwhelmed him – he watched helpless as she filled her own pipe load.

Little Willy's heart thrummed like an electric guitar, and every sound within and without him sounded as if he was inside a fifty-gallon steel barrel with angels drumming on the outside to deafen him in throbs of ecstasy. Every beat of his heart felt like an orgasm.

When Willy returned to reality, Marla was sagging back after her own hit and Ghost took the straight shooter.

"This pipe is too hot," Ghost said, laying it on the coffee table. "Come back to me Willy. Tell me about Speedy again."

There was a knock on the door. Ghost unfolded his gangly length, stepped over and leaned his head over to listen at the door.

"It's me. Sherri," came through the door.

Ghost opened and Sherri scuttled in. She squatted next to Willy, flipping her hair back over one shoulder. She ogled the rocks on the table.

Ghost pressed the ball of his knobbly thumb on the rock Willy had already been chipping off, bearing down until half the golf ball disintegrated into smaller chunks. Ghost picked up one huge specimen and put it on the end of the pipe, where it sizzled and melted into the hot filter as he handed it to her.

Sherri simpered at Little Willy. "You want me to stay after, Willy? You know this hubba makes all the girls horny."

She planted one hand on his crotch and gave a squeeze, but Willy's johnson was a limp noodle after as long a crack run as he had been on.

Sherri sucked on the pipe strong and relentless. The straight shooter flowed solid white with smoke despite her deepest inhalation. When her lungs were full, she stopped hitting to cough voluminous clouds of white into the already smoky hotel room. Willy, Ghost, and Marla leaned forward; nostrils flared as if to inhale her wasteful secondhand smoke.

Sherri's eyes rolled up in her head and she went into convulsions. She slumped over sideways and fell full length to the cheap carpet with a thud. She shuddered in a jiggering piston motion, with only the whites of her eyes showing. Sherri's mouth was open and drool dripped out onto the floor. Her paroxysms stopped and she lay still.

Willy squirmed in his seat. "Shouldn't we. . ."

Marla had spent this whole time enjoying her own short lived high with drooping eyes but returned from la-la-land.

"She's got to be gone," Marla said. "She has to be elsewhere, now."

Ghost tilted his head to the side and stared into space, nodding as if he were listening to a conversation only he could hear. He untied his hoodie and tossed it back, exposing a medusa mop of matted hair. He picked up Sherri's limp weight effortlessly.

One of Sherri's arms hung limp, escaping the circle of his embrace to point at the floor. By coincidence, her outstretched index finger made it appear as if the comatose crack whore was pointing down at the way to hell.

Marla scuttled to the hallway door, opened it a crack to peer out all wide-eyed. Ghost stepped into the hall with Sherri in his arms.

Down the hall a hatch with a handle at the top was inset in the wall. The hatch opened like a mailbox so garbage could be dumped inside to fall several stories down the chute into a dumpster in the basement.

Willy followed Ghost to the hatch. Marla leaned around the corner of the doorway goggle-eyed. Fogbanks of crack smoke spilled out Marla's door to spread across the hall.

"Open the hatch, Willy," Ghost said. His calm voice exuded patience.

Sherri's right eyelid was fluttering. Willy took a step back. Ghost tossed Sherri onto one shoulder and opened the hatch. Willy returned to the room and pushed inside past Marla.

"I'm disappointed in you, Willy," Ghost said from out in the hall. "Speedy would have helped."

Little Willy heard the rustling thump of Sherri's body being crammed into the chute. The corpse boomed and slithered and crashed against the walls of the chute all the way down to the splat of Sherri hitting bottom.

Willy put his rock-and-a-half in his pocket. Marla grabbed the pipe and swept the chunks of broken-up rock toward her with the edge of her hand. She rubbed her palm all over the coffee table and licked it clean.

She put a rock in the pipe, and the torch shook in her hand as she took her hit. The torch spilled from her grasp to clatter on the table as she leaned forward in a swooning rush, covering her stash with her free hand.

Little Willy started toward the doorway. Before he reached it, he stopped cold. His .45 materialized in his hand.

"Ghost," Willy said to the empty doorway. "If you're waiting right outside the door, I won't take it kindly."

He racked the slide to strip a round into the pipe: Klik-klak.

Ghost said, "Leave."

Willy stuck his head out the door with the pistol held back along his leg. Ghost stood by the garbage chute giving him that silent stare, his unkempt mane of tangled hair framing his wedge of a visage.

Little Willy rushed out the door and scrambled backward away from Ghost, his gun pointed at the rangy man's hatchet face. Ghost lurked by the chute, his air of spiritual deformity more blatant than usual. He gazed intently after Willy like he was taking a psychic photograph.

The door to Marla's room was still open and crack smoke still billowed into the hall. Although he could not see inside there, Little Willy heard Marla abusing the torch and gulping hits right up until he slammed through the exit door at the end of the hall and commenced booking down the stairwell.

3: FAT BOB PAYS THE RENT

Sure Fat Bob was running late, but so what? It was hard enough finding parking in the City without anyone pitching a bitch about it.

Fat Bob snagged a spot on Columbus and then marched downhill and around the corner onto Broadway. The red lights and neon of North Beach San Francisco surrounded him.

The titty bars were in full swing as Bob passed. The Condor Club advertised 'Carol Doda Completely Nude.' Next to that was Big Al's, then The Roaring 20s, and then the Hungry I with its 'totally topless college coeds.' Hucksters stood outside each strip club like animate wooden dummies, barking with hoarse voices, beckoning all and sundry inside.

It was a varied crowd clogging the sidewalks in front of the On Broadway and the Mabuhay Gardens next door to it: swaggering skinheads, mohawkers in spike-studded leathers, hard-core punkers and assorted derelicts and proles.

Across the street a mob of head bangers skulked around outside the Stone; Y&T was headlining. Metallica, some garage band of thrash-metallers out of El Cerrito, was the opener.

Fat Bob was working the On Broadway tonight rather than the Mab. He wended his way through the crowd to the club entrance.

Those who knew the short stump of a man tended to move out of his way with a nod of greeting, or a 'Hey, Bob.' Those who did not know Bob moved anyway when they got a good gander at this bullet-head's scar-mottled face. When they noticed just how hella thick and wide his rolling shoulders were in relation to his short stature, just how big his veiny paws were, jutting out the sleeves of his Derby jacket.

Fat Bob fell into position next to the ticket booth and started his shift: checking I.D.s on the people lined up at the door, stamping the hands of those old enough to drink, and scanning the growing crowd for troublemakers.

Fat Bob confiscated several phony I.D.s and refused entrance to one belligerent drunk before he shut down the ticket window and moved inside. Smegmella, the warm-up band, was commencing their set as Bob mounted the steep narrow flight of stairs into the club.

Blue clouds of tobacco smoke filled the air, and the waxen burnt crayon stench of clove cigarettes. Up on the horseshoe-shaped balcony, running in a half circle around the inside of the room's second story.

Bellied up to the bar, Jello Biafra was deep in conversation with Ginger Coyote. As Bob walked past, Ginger threw her back her head and laughed at something Jello said. Next to them, Bob Noxious nursed a Dead Elvis, staring into his drink's luminous green depths; his harem of Fuckettes attended him.

Fat Bob checked the Big Room first: A halfhearted pit filled with Huntington Beach Stroll-ers swirled counter-clockwise in front of the floodlit stage.

There was a smaller girl's pit off to the side where the action was a little less intense: Two couples waged a piggyback battle with the girls shoving at each other from atop their boyfriends' shoulders. Mohawker chicks skipped around flailing their arms in exaggerated mosh movements, while others pogo-ed up and down.

Patrons crammed the booths at the edges of the room. Blue clouds of tobacco smoke filled the air, as well as the waxen burnt crayon stench of cloves.

Bash and his crew of skinz sat at a table: psychic clones with gleaming shaven skulls, red suspenders under bomber jackets and rolled up jean cuffs over Doc Martin boots. One skin was getting his ear pierced with a safety pin while his cronies passed around a bottle of amyl-nitrate.

Screwup stood in the corner, arms folded, resembling a shaved ape as usual. The skinhead was grim-faced and stony jawed as he watched the girl's pit and the rest of the Big Room.

He saw Fat Bob approaching and gave him the thumbs up. Bob bounced on his toes in time with the music as he stood next to Screwup, both men scanning the crowd.

"Who all's working?" Bob snapped his fingers to the beat.

"You. And me," Screwup said.

Fat Bob stopped grooving for a second, but then shrugged.

Smegmella was on its last number, and patrons packed the Big Room.

Bob skirted the main pit, which was a churning mass of thrashers slamming each other to the music. Occasional stage divers climbed up to posture in front of the band before leaping out into the audience, to be caught and passed around above the crowd's heads.

Screwup was still in the same spot with his back against the stage, watching over it all. Fat Bob left the Big Room, marching to the beat and grooving to the music as he continued his patrol.

The headliner band, the Bar Sharks, set up and did a cursory sound check before beginning to play. As the band kicked off its first number a major pit formed in the Big Room. More people streamed to the center of the room, slam dancing into each other like maniacs to the chain-gun riffs, high off the lead singer's enraged vocals.

Fat Bob stopped nodding to the music as the expanding melee absorbed the girls' pit. Screwup charged from his corner but was swept into the core of the mob where Bob could no longer see him.

Someone raised the already deafening volume on the sound system to aching intensity. The band played harder and faster. And the audience went berserk.

In such close quarters, everyone in the pit bounced off each other like molecules in a pot of boiling water, pummeling and kicking while non-participants were pinned in the corners of the room.

STREET RAISED: THE BROKEN RIVER BOOKS EDITION

A topless girl flailed around with a roofing-nail-studded gauntlet, shredding shirts, and slicing open stomachs – a pudgy mohawker punched her in the jaw, knocking her down. The mob of thrashers kicked her unconscious body to the outer edges of the pit to join the other unmoving forms sprawled there.

Thrown bottles and pitchers were shattering throughout the room. Fat Bob ducked as a flying pint glass sailed past him to explode against the wall, close enough the glass shrapnel cut his cheek.

A tiny hot-eyed woman darted up to dab her fingers at the blood on his face, then leered at him as she licked her fingertips while stroking her crotch with her other hand.

"Blood," she screeched in joy.

She whirled away and the swirling mob swept her from sight. As Bob watched her disappear, he had no idea his own eyes were glowing as hot as hers.

Bash and his satellite skinz were back-to-back clubbing people with chairs. Some Polytech Punks used tables as battering rams, cutting swathes through the mob and knocking people down, crushing them against the wall.

A kid climbed on stage and dove off. The mob of slam dancers parted beneath him and he fell headfirst into the crowd, which closed over him. At least a dozen forms on the bloody floor now, not moving as the mob danced over and on them.

Bob bulled into the crowd toward the stage, tossing dancers to one side or the other. Random impacts rocked and buffeted him: punches and elbow smashes, kicks to the knees and ankles. It felt like he had fallen into a washer on spin-cycle.

A blow to Bob's temple left his ears ringing – someone snagged the front of his tee shirt and ripped it half-off from under his open jacket. An anonymous hand slapped against his face, its nails scoring another gash on his cheek as he jerked his head away from the probing thumb.

He was beneath the stage. The Bar Sharks' singer howled his message of anarchy to the microphone in a gargling series of belch-like vocals. Bob made the cut-off gesture to the singer, drawing his finger across his throat.

The singer grinned down at Bob, then turned to the band and pumped his fist up and down. The crowd brawled even harder in response as the band sped up.

Fat Bob climbed onstage. The singer recoiled when he saw the bouncer's eyes and dropped his microphone to backpedal away. The mike hit the stage boards with an amplified thump.

Fat Bob pulled out the power cord from the sound system. The music died in mid-note, and silence descended. The band members mouthed catcalls at him from out of reach – but the audience growled in sudden frustration, one beast with many throats.

Fat Bob stepped to the front of the stage and said loud as his throat-punch scarred vocal cords would allow: "The show – is OVER."

He panted and quivered, grinning wider and wider as he watched the faces of the mob gear up to destroy him.

The lights came on, revealing the club's current devastation and its innate tawdriness. Everyone appeared as if awakening from a dream, no longer able to hide in darkness' anarchic anonymity. Out in the crowd, Screwup worked his way toward Bob, bleeding with countless small wounds.

"You heard him," Screwup yelled. "This bar is closed. You can go wherever you want, but you cannot stay here. Now police up your friends and head on."

The mob heart cracked, the spell of the crowd-mind was broken as they looked around at the injured and unconscious on the floor. The patrons gathered up their respective wounded and filtered out through the wreckage.

Bash flipped the bouncers off. He and his dog pack left along with the rest of the crowd filtering out through the wreckage.

Bob Noxious left too, escorted by his Fuckettes. Noxious had a couple extra pairs of Doc Martin boots in addition to the ones he wore, hanging by their laces around his neck.

Dirk Dirksen – the older European man that operated the On Broadway – stood at the entrance to the Big Room inspecting the damage as audience members filed past him.

Later, Fat Bob perched atop a stool at the bar, clutching his beer. A couple of empties lay on their side in front of him. The rags of his tee-shirt still hung down from under his jacket, although the blood had clotted on his cheek.

Screwup came out of the office and snagged a beer for himself. The skinhead handed Fat Bob a wad of bills, which Bob thumbed through carefully before sticking in his wallet.

Screwup sipped off his beer. "You heard?" Screwup asked. "Landlords are taking it all away. Once the On Broadway's gone, I'll have to bread-and-butter it bouncing the gay bars."

Screwup looked quizzically at Fat Bob's expression. "What, Bob? You got something against the gays?"

Screwup shrugged, took another sip off his beer. "You'll be looking me up then I bet – I can get us on at the Stud and the Manhole at least, and work is work. Speaking of which, there's a show in the Mission tomorrow night at the Tool & Die. I need another man to work the basement."

Fat Bob stopped rotating his bottle and squeezed it. He reached out to give one of the empties a spin.

"Why not?" Bob asked. "Miya needs new shoes, and Miranda sure ain't gonna buy 'em."

4: THE BOYS ARE BACK IN TOWN

As the Corvette exited the Nimitz down the 29th Street exit off-ramp, Speedy studied his reflection on the inside of the passenger window. He moved his face around, considering his mirror image from various angles against the backdrop of the night outside. He had the Doberman face of a freckled Lee Marvin with flaming shoulder length red hair, wearing a surplus field jacket over a tie-dyed t-shirt.

For better or worse, he looked like what he was: a savage motherfucker.

The car pulled over. Speedy thanked the driver for the ride and got out at Elmwood & Derby.

He followed Fruitvale under the freeway and the elevated BART tracks, inland toward Clinica de la Raza. The smell of chili and grilled onions from Doggie Diner competed with the odor of sugar and hot greasy dough from Winchell's. Mariachi spilled out El Gato Negro's open door and car clubbers cruised back and forth on East 14th along the traditional route.

He turned the corner west on East 14th, heading away from the Dirty 30s and toward the Twomps. Up ahead by the abandoned Monkey Wards was a neon bar sign: The Pandemonium Bar & Grill.

As he approached the entrance a woman came out: a wiry Black girl with a magnificent rack displayed to advantage. She did a theatrical double take when she saw him.

"Hello, gorgeous," Miranda said, with that Mona Lisa smile of hers. "Still mad at me?

Speedy said, "I lost count of how many times I laid in my bunk trying to think of the perfect thing to say when we met."

"What did you come up with?"

"Nothing suitable. Just a bunch of half assed one-liners without any real zing to 'em."

"Keep working on it, cow poke. You'll produce something worthy of the situation. Something biting and cruel, as is your way."

"You know I'm looking for your brother. Throw me that bone at least, Miranda."

"You're still a workaholic, Speedy. He's bobbing up and down with the tide somewhere. Maybe I'll tell him you're around. Maybe he'll get back to you." She brushed one of her perfect breasts against his arm as she walked past.

Speedy watched her ass closely as she strutted away and hopped in a cab. He entered the bar but froze as soon as he walked through the door.

Ferns and Tiffany lamps hung from the ceiling. Framed mirrors covered the walls. Something low and sultry played on the jukebox. A sweeping length of polished mahogany served as the bar. Upscale couples nibbled on exotic drinks, well dressed in glaring contrast to Speedy's thrift store chic.

The bartender wore a tee-shirt with iron-on letters spelling 'Benny' under an Oakland A's baseball uniform shirt. He beckoned Speedy over. Speedy bellied up to the bar.

Benny still had his silver-and-black-attack Oakland Raiders plaque next to the cash register – only now there was a noose hanging in front of the plaque. A piece of paper was taped to the noose, inscribed 'Reserved for the Godfather, "Mister" Al Davis.'

The bartender's observant eyes belied his bland expression. His gaze flicked past Speedy to the door.

Speedy smiled. "Yeah, I saw Miranda on her way out. If I didn't use the baseball bat on her the night we broke up, I'm not about to bloody your sidewalk tonight."

"I'm sure you two will reach an understanding," the bartender said. "You were made for each other and then someone burned down the factory. The place a little different than you remember?"

"Well, I miss the saw dust on the floor."

"I don't. I needed a dustpan to scoop it up when you clumsy lads bled on it. And when it'd been vomited on? You don't wanna know."

A beer materialized in front of Speedy and he reached for his wad.

The bartender shook his head. "First one after raising is on the house."

"Thanks, Benny. So what happened to Bad Will?"

"The cops figure there must have been a robbery. Leastways the safe was cleaned out when I discovered his body." Benny shrugged. "I bought the place with some money I inherited around then. As you see I've spruced the dive up.

"It pulls down some nice ducats now." Benny gave him a lopsided grin. "No offense, gunslinger – but you and the guys were cheapskates between scores. You'd all huddle over your nickels then, like freaking squirrels with their nuts. Speaking of which, you left quite the tab here when you took your fall."

"I'll cover my marker soon as I'm flush, O greedy one." Speedy turned his back to the bar and rested his elbows on it.

Every man but Speedy sported nice haircuts and expensive clothes. Couples were chatting each other up, and women were laughing at private jokes he would never share. He turned back to face the bar, huddling over his beer.

Thin Lizzy came on the jukebox, 'The Boys are Back in Town.' A blast from the past about home fries reunited. About lost wild boys returning home and reclaiming their glory days to universal adulation and acclaim.

Speedy's cheeks commenced a slow burn. He studied the tiny bubbles rising in his beer intently as he listened close to the song's lyrics, the whole way through.

5: LIFE OF THE PARTY

Fat Bob's sister Miranda lived on the Alameda side of the Park Street drawbridge. As Bob exited the car, fog blurred the boatyards and brick warehouses lining the Estuary. Mist softened the outlines of the old houses, perched Riviera-like on the Estuary's edge amongst the marinas and snaggle-toothed rotting piers.

Fat Bob entered the apartment, shut and locked the door. He still had dried blood on his cheek, and the rags of his half-torn-off t-shirt still dangled down out the front of his jacket.

Miranda sat at the kitchenette counter in front of a lighted makeup mirror. Her black & white portable TV was tuned to Soul Beat on Channel 20. She was naked from the waist up, dressed only in a skintight lycra miniskirt.

She dusted her chocolate breasts with rouge, using a horsehair brush. Fat Bob refused to watch her, instead eying the portable. Night Dog was on – as always, the brother was getting heckled and roasted on by a phone caller.

"'Bout frickin' time," Miranda said, not turning away from her magnified reflection in the mirror. "I need the car for an outcall, and I need you to watch Miya. Carmel just left; she has an early class."

Fat Bob took the wad of bills from his pocket and tossed it on the counter. His sister pounced on the money, counting it with squirrel quickness before making it disappear.

"It's short," she said.

Fat Bob spoke in the permanent rasp caused by being punched in the throat one too many times. "I was hoping to take Miya to Children's Fairyland and buy her some pink popcorn. Maybe treat us to Fenton's after."

"Rent's due, Bob. Take her to Train Park. It's free."

Fat Bob handed Miranda the leavings of his wad, and she put it away before returning her gaze to the mirror. She brought her shoulders forward, emphasizing her cleavage, experimenting with a simpering pout as she admired her beautiful doppelganger.

"My big, badass brother," Miranda said. "Surfing on my couch."

Bob sat on the center of said sofa and began unlacing his Doc Martins.

Miranda flicked her gaze at him and away. "Guess who I saw at the Pandemonium? Speedy just raised; he's back in town and looking for you."

She applied eyeliner with the skill of a heart surgeon. "He's smoking hot as ever, I must say. The fool looked like he can't decide whether he wants to screw me or make soup out of my bones."

Bob crammed his feet back into his Docs.

"Who's going to watch Miya?" his sister screamed as he headed out.

Bob stopped in the doorway and glowered at her from under brows beetled so hard they hurt. He took a breath to speak but shut his mouth when he saw his niece standing in the unlit hallway leading to her room.

Miya was darker than her Uncle Robert but lighter than her mother. The little girl somberly watched the exchange.

Bob said, "You be here when I come back, Miranda."

The obnoxious look was still pasted on Miranda's mug – but her eyes flickered back and forth above the mask. Bob let her sweat for a moment before heading out.

Fat Bob slammed the Pandemonium's door against the wall hard enough to rattle the mirrors nearest the entrance and make the hanging ferns dance. WHAM's 'Careless Whisper' played on the jukebox, but the mating dance came to a halt as the drinking couples shut their yaps and stared. Bob stood in the doorway, a Neanderthal Nemesis.

Speedy was at the bar, and Fat Bob rolled up to engulf his

skinnier, taller blood brother in a bear hug. Benny poured three shots of Jameson's, ignoring impatient patrons.

"Here's to the days when this was a meat eater's bar," Benny said, lifting his glass. The three men downed their shots.

A drunk wobbled their way. "I was waiting before this bum. Who do I have to blow to get some service in this dump?"

"Keep your pants on, boss," Benny said.

Fat Bob strolled past the drunk and smashed a fist upside his head. The drunk slammed into the bar and sagged in a heap by the brass rail.

Bob hovered over him, bouncing on his toes. "See what happens when you badmouth my friend?"

Fat Bob gave the bar patrons a bow and they headed for the street.

"Don't come back now, hear?" Benny said as they left. "At least not 'til tomorrow. I'll make frou-frou drinks for ya, little umbrellas and everything."

When they hit the bricks, a police cruiser sat parked at the curb. A gold tooth glinted as the burly black driver grinned. The cruiser door opened and he climbed out, grunting.

The police officer's collar was buttoned, but the burn scars were still visible: crawling up his neck and the side of his face to the shiny bald patches on his scalp where hair would never grow again.

Speedy studied the police officer, seeing the ravages of time. The beer keg belly sticking out and almost hiding the pair of sap gloves tucked into his belt – the belly at least had not been there last time.

"Assume the position, white boy," Officer Louis instructed Speedy. The police officer smiled at Fat Bob. "You too, sweetie."

Speedy and Bob turned to face the exterior of the bar and placed their hands against the wall with feet spread and angled back so they leaned.

"Strangest thing," Louis told Speedy as he commenced a pat down. "Just saw a car full of sketchy boys roll up, but they peeled out when they saw my roller. I can't be the only one knowing this would be your first stop."

"Welcoming venues are a little sparse for me at present," Speedy told the wall a foot from his face.

Louis ran his hand up the inside of Speedy's leg, stopping well short of the jewels. "Little Willy walked away clean; don't try to claim I didn't hold to my end. It's like you were trying for suicide-by-street after Miranda did you like that."

Louis went through the motions of searching Fat Bob as well. Bob's face was pinched and livid. As Officer Louis laid hands on him, he smiled at Bob's quivering rage. "Give my regards to your sister, huh Bob?"

Officer Louis keyed his shoulder mike. "Adam Nine Code Four."

The mike squawked and hissed: "Nine, Code Four, copy." The woman dispatcher's voice was melodious, and Speedy found himself wondering just what she looked like, and if she put out.

Louis winked at Speedy. "That's a negative on the disturbance complaint, both RP and suspects were GOA upon my Four."

"Copy that Nine," the dispatcher said. "Advise when no longer Code Six."

"Okay," Louis told Speedy and Bob, rubbing his big, calloused hands together with a sound like mating sheets of sandpaper. "I'm cutting you mutts loose. Go and sin no more. Or at least as little as possible whilst I'm in eyeshot."

The fat old cop drove off to continue his patrol alone. As this was another year wherein Oakland was Murder Capital of the USA, it promised to be a busy tour for him.

"Pig," Fat Bob said, after Louis was well out of earshot. "Did he really cry like a bitch when those doofuses got acquitted? Wish I'd been in the courtroom with you to see it. C'mon, I borrowed Miranda's Valiant."

Speedy and Bob headed down East 14th in the direction of the 'Oakland is Proud' mural. They came up on a dozen teenage cholos walking in front of them, clogging the sidewalk from storefront to gutter.

The majority dressed in 'the Style:' wearing fedoras or bandanas down over their eyes, Pendleton shirts with the top buttons buttoned; Ben Davis pants or starched razor-creased khaki trousers, with spit-shined Stacy Adams kicks on their feet.

Most were Latino, but there was one black-skinned mayate and a couple of red-headed hueros. The white and Black kids were the most faithful to cholo style in their dress.

The Eses strolled at a snail's pace, about half-a-mile an hour. They were cool and oblivious even as Speedy and Bob piled up on their heels and were forced to slow to their speed.

"Ex-CUSE me," Bob bellowed in a fruity voice made even more sarcastic by its gargling roughness.

The little gangbangers turned their heads to face them, with shocked expressions. A couple reached under their Pendletons and Speedy stuck his hand in his pocket to grab his foldie.

Like a school of fish parting to stream around a reef, the crowd of little Eses split to allow them passage. Not meeting any of their eyes but not letting go of his foldie either, Speedy kept his gaze on the pavement the whole way through the group. Bob, however, sneered at everyone and no one as they cut through.

On the other side of the gangbangers the two men picked up speed and left the Eses behind. The boys resumed their crawl of a parade, none of them looking at Speedy or Bob, none of the crowd even acknowledging the rest of their own pack's existence as they strolled along in the direction of the Murder Dubs, staring at the sidewalk.

Fat Bob glanced back at them. "Somebody's gonna be in a major hurt locker before tonight is through."

"You know I need to find Little Willy," Speedy said.

"He's gone downhill while you been inside, man." Fat Bob said. "He's no more than a degenerate crack head now, hitting the bat pretty much nonstop."

"That's my little brother you've written off."

Bob pursed his lips. "Dreamer might know where he's cooping now. I don't pretend to."

Fat Bob turned off Fruitvale and crossed the tracks, passing low industrial buildings tagged with swathes of cryptic graffiti.

This was Jingletown, the 94601. Chickens free ranged the yards, which were filled with cacti and tropical plants. Avocado pits hung suspended on toothpicks in shot-glasses on kitchen windowsills. Food smells filled the air: the aroma of frijoles and tortillas that were never bought in a store. The eclectic choices in house paint colors were another clue you were in the J-T: purple, daiquiri, aqua, and much usage of yellow and black, Jingletown's colors.

Dreamer's house was on the Jingletown Riviera, on the Estuary next to the three big Sheds. Fat Bob had to drive half a block further to find parking as the cars of the other guests crowded the curb directly in front of the pad: hotrods, a couple low riders and customized pimp Cadillacs.

A row of Harleys dominated the lawn. East Bay Dragons milled about next to their hogs flying their colors: red on yellow, with the green dragon slithering in the middle.

The curtains were shut at Dreamer's house, but music and yelps of excitement spilled out the open front door. A dozen people stood on the front lawn drinking wine and passing around a joint or three. Two brawlers rolled around on the grass walloping each other whilst onlookers bawled encouragement. A couple leaned against the garage door swapping spit.

The two men walked through the front door into the party proper. A disco ball rotated on the ceiling and flecks of light crawled across the half dozen couples swaying in the middle of the living room with their crotches ground together hard. The air was thick with marijuana smoke.

Couches shoved against the walls were wedged full of people talking over Malo's 'Suavecito' which was playing on the turntable. Cholos and low-rider chicks constituted the majority, with a smattering of whites, and some Blacks. They were smoking hash or passing joints, swilling alcohol, or bowed over tooting lines. Each sofa had a coffee table in front, crowded with bottles of liquor and plastic cups of beer, baggies of weed, powder-strewn mirrors, and ashtrays crammed with cigarette butts.

Several folks exchanged nods of greeting with Speedy and Bob as the two approached Dreamer - a cholo with hairnet protecting his Eddie Munster coif, wearing a wife beater under his flannel shirt, khaki trousers and white knee-high socks with house slippers.

Dreamer held court next to a keg in a washbasin of ice.

"Suds time," Fat Bob said as he made a beeline for the beer.

Dreamer was smoking a blunt with a Black player in a kangol hat. Dreamer passed the joint to Speedy, who did a polite puff-puff-pass.

Fat Bob had finished his first beer and was pumping a second. If they stayed here long enough Bob would be doing keg handstand pushups and Speedy would have to drive designee without a license.

Dreamer said, "Speedy has raised, and returns to claim his hunting grounds." He smiled at the Black man and jerked his head at Speedy. "Look at him hanging back a little, like he's unsure of his welcome."

Speedy and Dreamer headed down the hallway into the depths of the house. A dim ruddy glow filled the hall from the naked red bulb overhead. The hallway continued past a closed door to the right, turning a corner at the end.

Dreamer opened the door on the right and they went in. He shut the door and threw the bolt. The broom closet sized 'office' was the same: a small desk minus a chair; a filing cabinet; and teetering stacks of miscellaneous items against the walls.

The two men gripped forearms and patted each other on the back while embracing; reflexively watching each other's six.

Dreamer said "Flor's passed out or she'd be cooking tamales right now, ese. Wrapped herself around a bottle of Tanqueray."

Speedy nodded. "I'll be tasting home cooking soon enough. Right now I'm naked except for a pocket foldie. I was hoping you'd cut me a huss for old time's sake."

Dreamer opened a filing cabinet drawer and pulled out a 12-gauge sawed-off. The barrels were so short that the ends of the shells stuck out the muzzles a fraction of an inch. The stock was cut down to pistol grip size and wrapped in friction tape.

Dreamer placed the gun and a handful of shells on the desk. "It's a proven piece," he said. "It's been blooded."

Speedy broke open the sawed-off to verify the load, then snapped it shut and put it in the pocket of his field jacket. He put the rest of the shells in the other pocket. To Dreamer, it appeared Speedy had grown inches taller in a matter of seconds.

Dreamer favored him with an appraising look. "So how you fixed to earn?"

"Well, I glommed case money on the way home from the can, so I'm not tapped. But I ain't got any irons in the fire at present."

"I'm brokering a couple might be up your alley," Dreamer said, his voice gone low even though they were the only ones there. "There's some cat down southwest what needs to be gone, and they're offering good money to make it happen. Weapons to be supplied, the rest need-to-know."

"Who's paying?" Speedy asked.

"I'm thinking Italians but they used a cutout so I can't be sure. Can't vouch for them if that's what you're asking."

Speedy pursed his lips. "So they hold a cattle call, reaching out to strange talent. That means they're looking for a throwaway and I wind up in a shallow grave in the desert, maybe right on top of the mark. Fuck that noise."

"Yeah, that job sounded kind of hinky to me, too. But you might be able to figure an angle if you're hard up enough."

"And of course you get your end off the top," Speedy said with a grin. "I know you'd never throw me under the bus, brother."

Dreamer looked at the floor a second before meeting Speedy's gaze again. "I only got one other thing cooking. I know this cat, he's flush. Just split with his old lady, but she got the kid. He's relocating out of the country big time and he wants someone to snatch his boy for him."

Dreamer hastened to say, "It's his real dad, he's got money to burn, and I'll tell you what: I've met his old lady and she's a royal bitch."

Speedy said, "That's bottom feeder work. Is everyone else pissed off at me? Are all the bridges burned?"

"You'll always have me, right? Once cash flows and deeds are done, they'll forget the past soon enough. I mean, Miranda..." Dreamer stopped short, looked at Speedy from under. "They know how a woman can get under a guy's skin, prompt him to craziness.

I'll tell you what: her being Fat Bob's sister is the only reason she was hands off."

"Seen Little Willy around?"

"Yeah. He's up off San Pablo in Edseltown, squatting in this shot-up abandoned crack house. It's burned and posted; you can't miss it. I heard tell he's cooping in the basement. He's not looking good, amigo."

Speedy grunted. "You haven't been selling him that shite, have you?"

"You know I would never do such a thing," the drug dealer said.

Dreamer laid his arm across Speedy's shoulders as they exited the office and started back toward the party. "Well hell homes, let's get back to the cervesa and the grifa, run you by the rucas and see about getting your dick wet."

Behind them, from around the corner of the hallway, a woman screamed. Dreamer's straight razor appeared in his hand and Speedy pulled his sawed-off as they turned to face that direction. Speedy stood behind Dreamer's shoulder.

Around the corner a door slammed against the wall. Three boys came round, one cramming himself back into his pants and zipping up on the run as he shouldered the other two from behind.

When the three saw Dreamer and Speedy confronting them, the trio skidded to a halt. Their eyes locked on the steel gleaming in the Mexican's hand, the oiled blue shotgun barrels jutting from Speedy's.

Speedy raised his sawed-off to aim in, and Dreamer leaned to the side to give him a clear shot.

Flor appeared behind the men, lurching around the corner crazy-eyed and shaking in a torn red lace negligee. By the bloody light from the overhead bulb she looked like a newly risen vampiress.

Flor pointed at the three strangers. "They fucked me, Dreamer. I thought it was you 'til I woke up all the way."

Speedy had aimed his sawed-off at the floor as soon as Flor loomed behind his targets. Noting the sawed-off was aimed away from them, the boy who had just zipped up leapt forward and kicked Dreamer in the groin. Dreamer hunched over, his face contorting as he took a wild swipe with his razor that the guy easily dodged.

The three bulldozed forward and bum-rushed past Dreamer and Speedy. Speedy managed to buffalo one of them upside the head with the sawed-off's barrel as they passed. This boy fell to the floor and lay twitching.

Flor gave throat to another scream, this one savage with rage and humiliation that her victimizers had punked her man, too.

The boys spilled out into the living room and slowed as they hit the crowd of dancers. Splotches of light crawled across everything and everyone from the disco ball overhead. Many of the partygoers had risen to their feet, and everyone stared at the two strangers. Men converged on them through the press.

The two stiff-armed people to both sides and charged for freedom. The one who had zipped up was in the lead.

A biker threw a heavy glass ashtray at the lead white boy's head, cigarette butts spewing out as it whirled through the air. The lead boy ducked out the way, then jumped onto a line of coffee tables and ran down the length of them, his friend close behind.

The lead rapist kicked bottles and glasses in the faces of the people on the couches, powder-laden mirrors crunching under his feet. People shielded their faces against the flying liquor and glass, crying out in anger and dismay as the spilled fluids soaked them.

The two leapt off the table's end and dodged out the front door. As he exited the house after, Speedy saw the pair had a slight lead on their twenty-or-so pursuers.

There was the crack of a small caliber pistol shot, and the trailing rapist turned to look back with dopey look on his face. He recovered and continued sprinting after his friend, who had already started his car, a red Firebird Trans-am.

The Black player in the Kangol hat was the shooter. He stopped to aim his .38 at the trailing rapist and fired another round.

The rapist cried out and sprawled full-length to the sidewalk, clutching his right buttock. He lay holding the bleeding hole in his ass cheek as he watched his friend floor the Firebird into a burnout.

"Garrett," he cried after the departing car.

'Garrett' bootlegged the sports car in a donut U-turn and gunned away and around the corner onto Glascock. The fallen rapist stared at the red taillights of the Firebird as it made its escape.

The mob caught up and swirled to surround him. Dreamer shoved people to either side and stared down at him.

The mob parted and Flor stalked through to join Dreamer. She held his straight razor, tapping the flat of the blade against her leg. The rapist pushed himself up onto his knees, knelt before Flor with hands pressed together.

"I didn't even touch you I swear," he said. "Please, I'm not the one that did it to you, it was Garrett. I promise I'll tell you where he lives."

"Of course you will," Dreamer said. "Bring him inside with the other."

Four men picked him up and carried him inside, following Dreamer. Flor beamed all around in pride before following her man, the flat of the razor still tapping against her leg as she shut the door. The rest of the crowd dispersed fast, people getting in their cars and peeling out.

"Think anyone will dime them?" Fat Bob asked.

"Maybe not," Speedy said. "Still, accessory would be a chickenshit beef for me to go down for, so soon after raising – let's vamoose."

6: SPIN THE BOTTLE

Willy hurried down San Pablo past Your Black Muslim Bakery. Inside, the two tired looking sisters behind the counter both had those Islamic scarves covering their hair. They eyed Willy's pale self warily as he walked by their door.

If Willy had not spent all his money on rock, he could have marched right in there and ordered 'One whole bean pie to go please.' They might have unbent when they saw his money, which would have been the right color at least.

But coulda woulda shoulda didn't cut it. He was broke and besides, his stomach was so shrunken he couldn't've handled a single slice.

Willy continued home past Saint Paul Primitive Baptist Church, past shooting galleries and corners clumped with hookers. Some of the working girls hooted and beckoned, most dismissed him as a broke dick with withering glances.

Little Willy stopped at the liquor store around the corner from his house to buy several cans of cat food. As the Sikh proprietor bagged them, Willy spotted a catnip mouse on display next to the register and held it up to show the Sikh. The Sikh rang that up as well.

Willy walked around the corner from the liquor store down a side street with its streetlights shot out. In the near distance, the sewing-machine tirade of an Uzi retorted to the T-Rex cough of a shotgun blast.

Willy's house was halfway down the block, posted as condemned and boarded up. A gaping flame-blackened hole in the roof exposed the entire ground floor. The surviving walls were riddled with the bullet holes of multiple drive-bys.

From down the block came the harsh tinkle of broken glass followed by angry voices. Willy glanced that way, drawing his .45 and holding it down along his leg as he ducked into the backyard,

"Here kitty kitty kitty," Willy said as he looked around the shadowed yard.

He made clicking noises with his tongue against his teeth; pursed his lips and made a squeaking. Willy descended the basement steps, pushed open the piece of plywood serving as a door, and slipped into the waiting darkness.

The only illumination was the dim light spilling in past the open plywood door. He set the .45 and the bag of cat food on the workbench.

He faced the darkened area of the basement and stomped his feet repeatedly. He smiled at the rustling and squeaking of a multitude of departing rats.

Willy lit a match which did not expose the furthest corners of the basement. Shadows boiled back there as the rats scurried away in their practiced time-share exchange. There was something in the middle of the floor but the match went out before he could identify it.

Willy lit a candle and held it up. The remains of a kitten lay in the middle of the floor, surrounded by a multitude of rat prints tracked in blood. All that remained of the cat was its intact head and one front leg, ending in a bloody tatter of stiff matted fur.

Willy picked up kitty kitty kitty by its remaining paw and carried it to his toilet bucket. There was a turd in the bucket. The kitten's carcass went *plop* as it hit bottom.

Willy flung the bag of cat food out the door. He put the plywood back in place, bracing it with a couple of two-by-fours.

He leaned against the workbench and looked around his basement domain: the workbench next to the door filled with tottering stacks of books. A barstool was the only chair. A plywood coffin-sized niche was inset in the wall – there was a greasy sleeping bag in there atop a half-deflated air mattress. Snowdrifts of dirty clothes carpeted the cement floor, and a burlap sack of canned goods hung from a rafter out of the rats' reach.

Willy laid his .45 on the workbench and gave it a twirl. Spin the bottle. The automatic rotated on its side, doing 360s.

It was pointing away from him when it stopped spinning. How many times would he have to spin it, to have it finally point at himself?

His face started to sag into one of his fugue states, but he caught himself in time and his expression hardened. He began laughing – but the tears flowed so profusely from his fearful eyes that it was hard to tell his laughter from lament.

From outside came a voice: "Hello, the house. This is Speedy out here. I'm looking for my brother Willy. If you're him, coolness. Otherwise, no beef and we fade."

Little Willy wrestled the plywood aside. Speedy looked past Willy into the basement. Speedy's brows rose as he saw the bloody rat footprints. His attention was drawn to Willy's sleeping bag which was sprinkled with rat droppings which slugs were eating.

Speedy recoiled. "Is this all you got, Willy?"

Little Willy had a tough time looking at anyone. "Well I had more, but it's over on the Island. I was sharing a house with a pot dealer there. You know Bash, him and his boys hang up at Dildo's in the Loin? Bash moved in and just took over, like. My roommate TJ told me he was tired of my raggedy ass, and Bash would give him twice what I was paying to deal from there. So he kicked me out."

Speedy scowled. "You didn't tell Bash to step off? You just let TJ punk you? Hell Willy, why didn't you get Fat Bob?"

"I'll wait in the car," Bob said, and walked away.

"Golly gee willickers," Willy said. "I fouled it all up. Huh sarge?"

Speedy grabbed Willy by the back of the head and pulled his face close, touched foreheads. "Unacceptable Willy. Let's get your crap back."

7: RAT BANQUET

As soon as Little Willy bailed out the exit, Ghost went down the hall after him. Ghost's long gangly legs took great strides as he pulled up his hoodie and cinched it tight around his face. Marla was still gulping crack smoke and her door was still wide open as Ghost hit the stairwell and descended.

When Ghost exited Marla's apartment building, Willy was nowhere in sight. Fog obscured his vision. From the direction of San Pablo Avenue came the distant sounds of a bamboo flute.

Ghost cinched the hoodie of his sweatshirt even tighter and started after Sherman past the Hygenic Dog Food Company. He was sonar-driven, homing in on the echoing notes of Sherman's distant flute through the all-encompassing white. Submarine warfare. Even as tall and lanky as he was, he moved without noise, sweeping down the sidewalk with silent majesty.

The notes of Sherman's flute came ever louder and less distorted from bouncing off the interposing buildings through the sea-smelling fog. He saw Sherman straight ahead, blurred by the fog but visible in the haloed glow of an overhead streetlight. Sherman's shoulders bulked wide under the orange leather of his jacket. Ghost lengthened his already long stride, gliding closer as he undid his hoodie and let it fall to his shoulders.

They were midway between two streetlights. He crept up behind Sherman, timing his breathing to Sherman's, walking in step with Sherman until he got close enough and then POW! Torpedoes in the water.

Ghost wrapped an arm around Sherman's throat from behind and hoisted him off the ground and choked him as his alligator shoes dangled and kicked at the air, his fingernails ripping and scrabbling at Ghost's sinewy forearm until he stopped struggling. Ghost gave Sherman's neck a finishing wrench, heard that *pop* of the cervical vertebrae dislocating, and laid Sherman's corpse down.

A warm wetness dripped down Ghost's forearm. Holding it up, he saw he was bleeding – Sherman's clawing had raked out runnels of flesh.

Ghost's forearm was also dripping with activator and moisturizer from Sherman's jheri curls. He whipped his arm at the ground, blood and jheri-juice flying off and spattering the sidewalk.

Ghost squatted for a better look, fascinated by the patterns the splattered drops made. The blood hypnotized him, shining black under the dim light of the distant streetlamp.

Sherman was a sleeping doll lying ever so peaceful. Ghost searched him, pocketed his stash and his money. He arranged Sherman's belongings next to his body in a pretty array: the bamboo flute, photos of smiling black faces, a stick of gum, and the eternal optimism of an out-of-date condom.

Ghost studied Sherman's things spread out like that. He touched them and rearranged them in different orders; wearing Sherman's taped up glasses.

He hit the neighborhood liquor store. Ghost walked the aisles with arms outstretched and fingers fluttering against the racked products on either side. He had the hoodie of his sweatshirt back up, the drawstring pulled so tight that he could only see out of a little sphincter-hole in front of one eye.

Ghost picked out some Freeze Pops and Ho-Hos – he was a sucker for them – and walked past the Sikh without stopping to pay. The Sikh's hand disappeared under the counter.

Ghost turned to face him. "I can smell you laughing at my pain from here."

The Sikh slowly placed both hands on the counter and Ghost left.

Ghost loosened his hoodie enough to see with both eyes once he was outside. He walked to the corner and was about to cross

San Pablo when he slowly rotated in place to look down the street behind him. Down the block across from the Elementary School, he saw Speedy, Little Willy and Fat Bob getting into a green Valiant.

Speedy saw someone coming toward them from the corner: a tree-like angular man in a sweatshirt with hoodie up and snug around his face. The guy was more akin to a machine rolling toward them on wheels, some sort of geared clockwork apparatus instead of a living, breathing human being.

Speedy interposed himself between his little brother and the stranger. Fat Bob moved out to the guy's side at 90 degrees to Speedy so they had him in a 'box,' one of them ready to slam him no matter which way he faced his guard. Ghost stopped, unconcerned by their flanking, threatening postures.

"You showed me where you live Willy," Ghost said. "That's not fun."

"Something?" Speedy asked.

On Ghost's blind side, Bob bounced on the balls of his feet and growled.

Ghost studied Speedy with an intensity. "Who are you claiming to be?"

Little Willy said, "Ghost, this is my brother, Speedy."

Something resembling excitement entered Ghost's voice. "Aha. Willy told me all about you. You're strong and heartless. Not weak like the Others."

"Sometimes Willy talks too much. I ain't looking for a fan club." Speedy observed Ghost's dilated pupils: smelled the same hubba stench off him that Willy reeked of.

"It's important that I'm meeting you," Ghost said. "We will talk one way or the other."

Speedy shrugged. "I already got a crew. No vacancy, get it?"

Ghost stepped in with one hand lifted, and Speedy had to take a step back to maintain his space. Fat Bob moved in to give Ghost the chop but Speedy waved him off with a look of revulsion in his eyes.

Speedy said, "Buddy, you stink like fish on ice. I don't know you,

I don't want to know you, and if you get my brother high again, I'll kill you. Now step off or make your play."

Ghost's face was still and expressionless as he continued staring silently at Speedy for some little time. He floated past them and was gone up the street.

"What the hell you have dealings with a freak like that for?" Fat Bob asked.

"It ain't like you were around," Little Willy said. "And Ghost ain't so bad once you get used to him."

After the Valiant left, Ghost doubled back around the corner, drifted into the backyard and down to the basement.

The candle still burned on the work bench. In the flickering light, he saw the rat droppings on Willy's sleeping bag. He saw the hundreds of bloody rat footprints circling the center of the basement.

He rotated slowly in place with arms extended, smiling. "Our Lady of the Rats," he intoned in a melodic voice.

He stopped rotating and sniffed. He walked around the pattern of rat prints, taking care not to step on the blood and mar the pattern. Ghost leaned over to take a careful peek inside Willy's toilet bucket.

He saw what was left of the kitten, embedded in human feces. Two big familiar looking rocks of cocaine lay embedded in the shit next to the dead cat.

Ghost leaned back and crowed softly with delight.

He headed inland. In that direction, the lights of high and mighty houses shone down from the wealthier Berkeley Uplands. Ghost walked that way, allowing feelings to creep out and dominate his face.

As he walked across an intersection through an increasingly hoity-toity neighborhood, a Land Rover pulled up at the stop sign next to him, mother and child within.

The child – a two-year-old girl named Nicole – saw Ghost's profile and whimpered. "Mama. That man, Mama. That man right there."

"Be quiet," Mama said, her own voice choked with fear.

Mama's eyes were as wide as Nicole's. She saw the turmoil infesting Ghost and sat frozen, her foot unable to step on the gas, her hands clenched hard enough on the steering wheel to whiten her knuckles.

Ghost continued, oblivious – though he would have made their acquaintance if he had noticed them, their terror would have been too delightful to pass up.

He walked with his head down, muttering obscenities in a conversation with invisibles: "...I'm sick of you changing everything while my back is turned, you can't fool me anymore, fuckers. Something important and special is about to happen, I'll finally find the way through. Yes, I know Willy is too flawed for the work. No. Shit. Don't say that. Speedy can't really mean it..."

He disappeared into the night after he left the illumination of the Land Rover's headlights. Shaking her paralysis away Mama floored it through the intersection, almost sideswiping parked cars before managing to straighten course. She did not let up on the gas until she was blocks away.

Mama and Nicole both slept poorly that night.

Ghost walked down the next side street, along a leaf strewn sidewalk that was little more than a tunnel through untrimmed shrubbery run rampant. He stopped and brooded, finally nodding as if in agreement with someone unseen.

He pushed through the jungle-like foliage between two houses to creep toward their backyards. He peeped over the fence it to examine the yard by moonlight before opening the gate and stepping through. He crept onto the back porch and tried the knob. Locked.

He checked over the next fence and then clambered over it. The next backdoor was locked as well.

In the next backyard he hit the jackpot: that porch door unlocked.

Inside, he tiptoed through the open bedroom door. A girl was on the bed. Ghost entered the room boldly.

She was in her twenties, wearing a teddy. Long, blonde hair

fanned out across her pillow, and her teeth gleamed pearly and phosphorescent between parted lips.

Ghost shut the curtains far enough to ensure privacy, but not far enough to block off the light from outside.

He untied his hoodie, pushed it back so his medusa locks sprang free. He leaned forward, letting his shadow slowly crawl up over her face; it covered her eyes, blocked the light spilling in from the street. Ghost waited, quivering.

Sensing the change in illumination even in her sleep, the girl's eyes opened. For an instant she stared at the ceiling, blue eyes clouded with slumber. As her wakening gaze rolled toward the backlit silhouette looming over her, and full awareness entered those beautiful orbs – Ghost smiled down at her.

8: WILLY'S BIG MOVING DAY

Speedy and Little Willy exited the Valiant. Fat Bob got his Louisville Slugger from the trunk, trembling like a hunting dog anticipating the taste of blood.

They were in a tree glutted white bread Alameda neighborhood, just off the Webster Strip. A black rattle canned Econoline van squatted in the driveway, sporting a KOME bumper sticker. They strolled past it and onto the porch of a slate-shingled house about the size of a postage stamp. The outside light was off.

Music leaked through the door: 'Revenge,' by Black Flag. Bob danced a constrained jig to the song, doing a two-step as he softly keened the lyrics. Speedy glanced at him and Bob stopped.

Speedy gave Willy a look. "Tell me you at least still got the door key."

Little Willy handed the key over.

Speedy drew the sawed-off from his jacket pocket. He pulled back both hammers and depressed the safety. He inserted the key in the lock and slowly worked the bolt.

Willy racked his .45 and held it down along his leg. Bob waggled his Louisville slugger. Speedy rotated the knob, pushed the door open and stepped inside.

"How do," he drawled.

Every head in the room whirled to face Speedy. Several skinheads leapt to their feet and loomed Speedy's way. They spotted the sawed-off and froze in tottering imbalance.

Bash sat in an easy chair. He had an AF tattoo on his neck; inked on his shaven skull was a corpse-worm burrowing in and out of his scalp. Bash's eyes widened as he saw Bob, and he fumbled inside his bomber jacket.

Speedy stuck his sawed-off against Bash's nose, breaking the skin. Bash's hand froze and he commenced to leak.

A boot woman, with her hair in a Chelsea feather cut, scuttled at Speedy with claws outstretched. "You killed my brother," she screamed. Speedy shoved his palm against her face and she flew back to crash against the wall.

Fat Bob followed Speedy in, moving to the left to 'make the box,' forcing everyone in the room to choose between his bat and Speedy's shotgun. With Speedy and Bob facing inward at 90-degree angles to each other, the marks could not focus on either without leaving themselves open to the other.

Willy shut the front door and leaned against it with his pistol in his hand. He looked around the manicured neighborhood: windows flickering with TV radiation, and wind kindly through the trees. Some unseen swab jockey barked like a dog, a few blocks over on Webster.

From inside through the door Willy heard strident conversation and muffled commotion, followed by the sound of a baseball bat hitting something meaty followed by a loud outcry. Willy giggled but went expressionless when the door opened.

The contrast between the nice neighborhood outside and the thrashed interior was surreal. The living room had been top-flight once, in keeping with the house's high-end exterior and the bedroom community neighborhood surrounding it. Now it was in the middle of a dedicated trashing as only skinz knew how to inflict: empties littered the floor and butts were ground into the carpet. Fist holes were punched into the walls, which were covered by racist comments, spray painted obscenities and bathroom stall artwork. Decks and long boards leaned in a row by the door. Someone had been smoking heroin; the room stank of the dragon.

Willy's roommate TJ, a pale little zombie in a katana coat, sat on the sofa subdued. His gaze bored holes in Willy, and he wore the victim's usual expression of surprise.

Other than TJ the room was skinheads and boot women only: a

half dozen stood or sat in the living room, beers and cigarettes in hand, most wearing Doc Martins like Bob.

Another boot woman with a cigarette dangling from her mouth was cooking a big pot of food bank spaghetti next to an overflowing trashcan. She turned off the gas and tapped the ash from her smoke. Next to her the sink was aheap with tottering stacks of dirty dishes green with mold.

A skin lay passed out on a stained mattress, buried in empty cans and bottles. From the look and smell of him, he had been pissed on.

A couple was screwing on another mattress, frozen in mid-stroke. The male was on top with his pants pulled down and his pallid buttocks exposed. They lay cheek to cheek staring at the newcomers.

Bash sat on the floor holding a swelling knee; blood from his gashed nose dripped off his chin. The feather cut girl knelt next to Bash. Her top was ripped down the front and her arms were crossed to keep her breasts from spilling out.

"You killed my brother in prison," she said. "You can't lie; everyone from the Loin to Bezerkeley knows it's true."

Speedy scowled. "What if I told you, it was self-defense? Let it lie."

"Tell me," She shouted. A yodeling tone of hysteria had entered her voice.

Speedy shrugged. "Your brother went punk bitch inside. He hit on me and I shot him down – I don't swing that way even in lockup. He took it poorly."

"Bullshit," she said. But her voice was weak; her flickering eyes would not meet Speedy's. One of the skinz turned his back. An Oi-Boy in a Tam hat reached out and tried to rest his hand on her shoulder but she slapped it away with a snarl.

The Oi-Boy turned his attention to Speedy. He wore a bomber jacket with Guinness and American Front patches on it; ruddy ham hock sideburns bracketed the shaved, oiled sides of his head under the tam.

The Oi-Boy moved to stand between Speedy and the Feathercut

Girl. "You only got two shots in that thing," Oi-Boy noted.

Speedy nodded. "Too true. One barrel in your direction for shits and giggles, the other toward whoever else is stupid enough to be a nuisance. This kind of spread, double-ought buck at point blank range into such a dense crowd? It'll be awful messy.

The Oi-Boy asked, "What'll you do after that?"

Speedy aimed in on his center mass. "What do you care friend? You won't be around to see it."

Fat Bob slapped his bat against his palm. Speedy stood as far from the marks as the wall would let him, holding the sawed-off at his waist with left palm resting atop the barrels. Little Willy searched person after person, putting the loot in a pillowcase.

The water from a broken bong dripped off the coffee table. A large baggie lay open in front of TJ, filled with a potpourri mix of Quaaludes and other scrips, next to a fist-sized rock of cocaine encased in saran wrap. Willy's gaze locked on the crack and he picked it up off the table.

Speedy said, "I'll take that. We'll dock my end for it if you like."

Willy handed it over. Speedy turned his attention to the skinz, who all now wore the expressions of people expecting the imminent departure of unwelcome guests. "Who belongs to the van? I'm thinking about taxing y'all, giving it to my baby brother for pain and suffering. But I want you gone so you get to keep it. Bash, you and your crew step off now."

The fucking couple covered up their junk, the passed-out lightweight was slapped and kicked awake, and the skinz scooped up their decks and slouched out the door. The Feather Cut Girl, pale and shivering, led the procession with Oi-Boy hovering as close as he could without physical contact.

Bash gimped along behind, the last to leave. As he headed out Bash studied them, memorizing their faces.

Speedy laughed. "You come back it'll get noisy. Don't be stupid, bo."

"That was pussy play at the On Broadway, Bob," Bash said. "You should have let us have our fun." He limped out.

TJ made as if to tentatively rise from his seat. "Not you, TJ,"

Speedy said. "Down boy."

Willy locked the front door and leaned against it. Speedy strolled to the easy chair and sat. Fat Bob turned off the stereo, stood behind Speedy and rested his bat on his shoulder.

TJ, slumped on the sofa, said "Thank you. You don't know them, they're awful. But they'll be back. You only chased them away for a little bit."

"I gave them their chance," Speedy said. "You should be more thinking about your own situation, dogging my brother around and all. Lucky for you I need a place to crash, and I nominate your crib. You see the stick, here's the carrot. You belong to the pot, right? Give him his stash, and his share of the cash."

Willy handed TJ's own stuff back to him.

Speedy said, "I want it to be business as usual for you. You'll barely even know we're here and we won't be underfoot that long. But if you pitch a bitch. Or worse, dime us to the Man?

"We got a deal?" Speedy asked. "This is the part where you indicate assent."

TJ almost broke his neck he nodded so hard.

Little Willy went back to his room in the back of the house. The scattered heaps of his belongings showed the cockroaches had rifled through it all. None of his books were missing, however – every tottering stack of first editions was still there, standing along the walls. A pair of soiled women's panties dangled atop one book pile – Willy plucked the underwear up between thumb and forefinger and tossed the unmentionables into the corner.

He flopped onto his bed and lay with both hands clasped behind his head; legs crossed as he smiled up at the ceiling. He would not have to keep one eye open for the rats tonight, and he would be able to drop his deuces in a real toilet. Speedy was back in town.

Coolness.

The next morning Speedy awoke and looked for sustenance.

Most of the kitchen cabinets were ripped from the walls, their remnants littering the floor. The pot of burnt food bank spaghetti sat congealed atop the sauce-spattered stove. The moldy dish piles in the sink stank. Speedy opened the fridge: nothing but rotting lunchmeat, crusty bottles of overage condiments, and half a six-pack of Coors Light. All he found in the one intact cabinet was a mostly empty box of Cap'n Crunch.

Speedy looked in Little Willy's door. Willy was sweating up a torrent. He thrashed and groaned. His lips pursed into sucking position and he made a deep inhalation like he was hitting a dreamland crack pipe.

Willy opened his eyes. "I can stand my own ground without you holding me up. But I'm not gonna rob anybody again, Speedy. I can't pretend to be you. I won't stick a gun in a man's face again unless they force me to."

Speedy considered. "We'll figure another way for you to contribute. You won't have to be utterly useless."

In the bathroom, the mirror was shattered, dried blood crusted the sink, and used needles littered the floor. Speedy examined the fist-sized rock of cocaine he had robbed from the skinz. It was worth thousands of dollars. He crushed it up and flushed it down the toilet.

9: DRINKAGE & CAGED FEMALES

That evening the boys bought beer and drove up to the East Bay Hills for drinkage. The crew opted for the southern portion of the Hills, down San Leandro way. The Valiant was parked atop the beetling grassy knob of Fairmont Ridge, downhill from the old Nike missile site.

Speedy and Fat Bob leaned against the hood with a case of beer at their feet. Little Willy prowled the outskirts amidst the shrubbery, muttering the Latin names of the plants he saw, taking great gulps of his beer every few seconds. He was restless and jumpy.

Behind them past a line of piss-smelling blue-gum eucalyptus trees, Lake Chabot glittered in the moonlight. In front of them sprawled the lights of the inner East Bay: down past County Juvenile Hall lay San Leandro, San Lorenzo, and the low lit-up San Mateo Bridge spanning the southern Bay's darkness to Foster City.

To the right and far across the Water, the lights of San Francisco glowed. Even at this distance the City was an ornate self-important visual shout. But that was the City, this was the Town.

"Alden and Remy got any scores they need extra hands for?" Speedy asked.

"Highly unlikely. They got in a shootout with some slangers down off 98th, caught one too many hollow points to swallow."

"How about Buzzkill? Still above ground?"

"Semi-buried. Our boy's doing all day and a night. Life Without for 187, just sentenced."

Bob finished his beer and tossed the empty in a long arc through the air. The Girls' Juvenile Hall was a long ways downhill but a tail wind lofted and carried the bottle so that after long seconds it smashed against the razor-wire topped fence surrounding the facility.

At the bottle's impact, the girls inside began screaming and catcalling up at the distant men, crying out for beer and telling the boys what they would do if they got their hands on them. Some of the promises were quite imaginative, others Speedy figured for physically impossible.

Speedy raised a beer in salute to his little caged sisters below. "A rowdy bunch."

"Rowdier than us, brother." Bob grinned.

"What about you Bob?" Speedy asked. "How'd you earn?"

"Doing pickup work mainly. Bouncing, body-guarding high rollers, gigs like that. I only robbed once but it went very, very bad. I'd prefer not to discuss the particulars."

"What about Joel and Lucky?"

"Well," Bob said, "They tried to rip off some Mexicans down in the Bottoms and got nailed. Those goddammotherfuckers wrapped Lucky and Joel up in chains and dumped them alive in the Russian River."

"I disliked those two less than some I could name," Speedy said.

Willy belched raspily and then retched. He dropped to his hands and knees by the underbrush at the edge of the turnout. He started ralphing, liquid garglings, as he vomited up the unaccustomed beer.

Fat Bob squatted by Little Willy's side and commenced patting him on the back.

"Get it all out, Willy," Bob crooned. "Puke that nasty garbage up, you worthless crack-head."

Willy let out with another ralph.

Speedy looked downhill at Girls' Juvie. On impulse he clutched the sawed-off in his field jacket and waggled it at them like a different sort of gun.

The captive peanut gallery went wild. Even from up on the Ridge he saw girls at the windows crying out for him to get his ass down there, girls' hands black, brown, and white beckoning from behind bars as they called.

The matrons rolled into the dorm, restoring order in what had become a near riot among all these sex-deprived teenage bad girls: so close to beer and boys, and yet so far. One of the matrons looked out the window at the three moonlit pervs silhouetted up on the Ridge. She turned her head to the side and spoke rapidly to someone out of sight.

"It's time to mosey along," Speedy said. "Hey Bob. How much money you think those Mexican cocksuckers have lying around?"

10: BIG ENOUGH IRON

The next morning, Fat Bob took Speedy past the lumberyards into the Lower Bottoms of West Oakland.

The double-decker elevated Cypress Freeway overshadowed the Bottoms. In the direction of the Water, cranes at Port of Oakland loomed behind the West Oakland skyline like Martian tripods.

Fat Bob parked in Ghosttown near the casket factories. He flashed his eyes at a house down the street with peeling scale-shingle walls, making it resemble a dragon with eczema.

Bob said, "That's their crib."

Speedy got out of the car. He meandered down the street toward the house, weaving increasingly the closer he got, 'til he was wavering on his feet when he reached the base of the porch steps. He continued the drunk act as he climbed the stairs.

"Michelle," he bawled.

As he reached the porch, the door opened to reveal two guards, both holding guns.

"Michelle," Speedy mumbled. "Want Michelle."

"Ain't no Michelle around here, rummy," the little guard said.

Speedy stole a glance past them at the interior. The front room spanned the width of the house, with an archway opening off the room into another open area further back. In the far room, a nattily dressed Mexican sat at a desk with his back to Speedy.

The Mexican turned in his chair to look at Speedy, revealing a pile of greenbacks on the desk – also a triple-beam scale, a money counter, and a taped-up plastic-wrapped brick of something-or-other.

Another man trudged up the porch steps behind Speedy to join the two door guards – a much bigger Latino dressed cowboy style and carrying a clinking bag of groceries. He inspected Speedy.

"You from around here?" the big Mexican asked, his voice kindly. "Not too many blancos in this 'hood."

"Bitch stole my money," Speedy said, not making eye contact, keeping his body and mind meek and stupid as he prepared to stumble down the porch steps and away.

The big Mexican stepped in front of Speedy, blocking his path. The Mexican looked up and down the block. Then he turned to Speedy and slapped the side of his head.

Speedy did not resist the blow, letting himself slam onto his side on the porch. He acted like it hurt worse than it did, he even wept crocodile tears as he moaned, "Where's Michelle?"

The Mexican's lips pressed together, unsuccessfully trying to hide a smirk as he turned to the two guards. "Get him the away from here."

"Sure thing, Oso," the smaller guard said.

Oso said, "Use my name in public one more time, puto."

The small puto cringed as Oso disappeared inside. The two guards started kicking Speedy, each getting out of the way to give the other his turn, each methodical kick heaving Speedy's body a little closer to the top of the stairs.

For the big guard it was just business, he did not put anymore into getting Speedy off the porch than he had to: he was more hooking his toes under Speedy and rolling him than anything else. The little guard, however, was paying Speedy back for Oso's humiliating words, really laying the boot.

Speedy covered up as best as he could; he gave them a little show, yelping a bit to satisfy their cruelty. But when he rolled off the top of the steps and bounced down to the sidewalk, he did not have to act to make it seem he was hurting.

He rose creakily to his hands and knees. The two guards went back inside.

Speedy got to his feet and continued the drunk routine back to Bob's car. He was sore enough that his limping hobble came semi-naturally.

"How's it look in there?" Fat Bob asked as Speedy climbed into the car.

"Beautiful fields of fire. All I need is big enough iron. Let's get Willy. I want his brain pan in on this."

Bob sighed. "I know Willy's your brother and all, but I could never figure out why you keep carrying him."

"He believed in me once, when I didn't."

11: SLAUGHTER AT SUNSET

The Valiant was parked by the boarded-up 16th Street Southern Pacific Station in West Oakland. It was dusk, and the sun was on the verge of setting. To their left – their north – the MacArthur connector ramps arced across the muck of the shore toward the Toll Plaza and the Bay Bridge. The Mud Flat Sculptures were barely visible on the far side of the freeway. A gate was open in the fence up that way, and a string of loaded railroad cars was rolling out through it with cargo from the Port.

Behind the Valiant – past razor wire and guard posts, past the warehouses and looming cranes of the Naval Supply Depot and the Army Base – lay soggy glistening wetlands and then the Bay.

Spanning the vista to their front and their right was the devastated landscape of the Bottoms – a raggedy grill of deserted houses, vacant lots, and dead blocks, with spaghetti-squiggles of railroad tracks leading nowhere embedded in the pot-holed streets.

But this wasteland was also interspersed with pockets of life: churches, light industrials, mom-n-pops, and houses as jealously maintained as any in the suburbs. The elevated Cypress Structure Freeway amputated the Bottoms from the rest of the Town.

Little Willy had not uttered a word the whole drive, just absorbing everything like a meat computer programming itself. Willy's unchanging expression of slack jawed fugue finally prompted Speedy to snap his fingers in front of Willy's nose. "Earth to Willy. Time to stop the home movies. Front and center, private."

Little Willy jolted from reverie.

"The Army Base and the Naval Supply Center block off the Bay side," Willy pointed out shyly. "The Bottoms are cut off from everything inland by the Cypress. The Man will throw up a surface street cordon first thing in hopes we're neighborhood punks."

Speedy nodded. "They'll isolate the Bottoms right off, with rollers at all the major intersections. Any units they use for local roadblocks are units we don't have to worry about chasing us, but we still got to be on the other side of the Cypress by the time they deploy."

"They'll have air on top of us inside a minute or two, max," Willy interjected. "Pig or newscaster chopper, doesn't matter. If they have even a partial vehicle description their choppers will pick us up easy. Then they'll deploy K-9s to flush us if we must bail from the car. We can't make the hit whilst there's a copter in sight."

Speedy said, "When they miss us with the initial cordon the Man will still expect us to be amateurs, hop on the freeway to get as far away as we can, as fast as we can. They'll swarm the Macarthur Maze and the Interchange. They might even shut down the Freeway if they coordinate fast enough with CHP."

"That's more units out of play, and gives us better options," Willy said. "We got Peralta, Adeline, Market or San Pablo if we want to bail north – West Grand or 14th Street if we head east. When they don't pick us up on the freeway the Man will like those main roads as much as we do. They can move fast along them and they'll have nice, long fields of view to spot us from a distance. We got to hit the back streets ASAP once we're free of the Bottoms."

"And then?" Fat Bob asked.

"And then we'll lie low at my old squat." Willy smiled apologetically. "It's on the far side of San Pablo, and it's right on the Edseltown border between Berkeley and North Oakland, so jurisdiction is murky. We zig, we zag, and we hunker down there for a bit. Once the first excitement's worn off, we move on when they think we're already long gone. It wouldn't hurt to have a swap-out vehicle stashed in case we're made at the drug house."

Speedy said, "So if we hit them fast and ferocious, don't get made by neighborhood eyewitnesses, don't get air on top of us before we're past the Cypress, and don't get spotted crossing any main drags, we get away clean."

Bob guffawed. "That's a lot of don'ts, but this just might fly. In my experience, folks in West Oakland hear a commotion going on down the block, their first response ain't to stick their noses out the door."

"Oh yeah?" Willy asked. He jerked his chin toward his left, in the direction of 34th and West Clawson. "Check this out; I was hoping we'd get to see it."

Dusk's gloom had settled in, but little Black kids stood around on various roofs over there, yelling and pointing at something in the direction of the Bay.

"Here they come," the distant voices piped in falsetto. "They're coming."

At first the three men in the car could not see anything. Then they sensed isolated, separated motion toward the water's edge – low slung creatures slinking inland through the growing darkness. A couple of streetlights popped on revealing what was creeping up on the child sentinels: dozens of stray dogs the color of the mud flats they had spawned in, emerging from the muck to raid West Clawson.

Hens kicked up a ruckus as a couple dogs hit a backyard chicken coop in the direction of the New California Barber Shop. From another backyard came the screams of a goat. A man came out on a porch with a hunting rifle and shot one of the dogs as a group raced by in the street; he worked his rifle's bolt, managing to drop another dog before that portion of the pack scattered. Around the way other firearms spoke: sounded like a couple pistols and a shotgun.

It was over seconds after it began. The surviving dogs loped back toward their mudflat dens, one of them with a bloody rooster dangling from its mouth. An injured dog howled in the gutter down by the House of God Spiritual Temple, taking its own sweet time to die. A man from a nearby house trotted out with an axe and finished the dog off.

"It happens every night and the cops don't do nothing," Willy said. "Hence West Clawson's real name: Dogtown."

Speedy looked around the neighborhood. "Then this is the time of day we hit them – when there's so much gunfire ours won't even stand out."

He smiled. "Bob's still right. We won't be here after their kids, or their livestock. This is a drug spat, a fire fight. They'll mind their business."

12: SLEEPING HORNET

The gate in the chain-link fence squealed as Fat Bob pushed it open and led the way up the walk. Speedy followed, his shadow. They were up by Macarthur/Broadway; the Valiant was parked by Mosswood Park, a few blocks away. Some old dudes in dashikis were playing conga drums at the park; drum rhythms were audible even from here.

A California Republic state flag hung upside down in the Baron's front picture window, serving as curtain; the golden bear on the flag looked like he was dead.

Some trailer park trash anthem played inside the house, the redneck singer going on and on about flirting with disaster. As they mounted the porch steps someone twitched back a curtain in the window next to the door, and the music switched off.

The door opened a little, and a man stood in the opening blocking Speedy's view of whatever lay beyond. The man's gray, thinning hair was drawn back into a ponytail. He was shirtless, exposing the physique of a tanned gymnast, with no body fat to blur his rippling muscles. Both his nipples were pierced with golden hoops.

Crude jailhouse tats covered his exposed upper body: the Vikings and swastikas and lightning bolts to be expected on any veteran white boy that had done a jolt of heavy time.

From the shoulders up the Baron was a much older man. The bones of his skull lay close to the surface, barely concealed by the tight-drawn seamed leather skin of his face. The whites of his eyes were as yellowed as the dead lawn in front of his house – this guy had the jaundice up, for sure.

"I thought you were coming by yourself," the Baron said,

speaking to Fat Bob but staring dead at Speedy.

"It's for me," Speedy said, staring right back at the Baron. "I don't buy any iron I ain't checked it out personally."

The older man looked past Speedy at the street. He stepped back out of their way. "Not on the porch, guys."

They entered, and the Baron shut and bolted the door behind them.

They were in what passed for a living room dominated by a half dismantled panhead. The tiny cubicle was littered with Harley parts and the portion not taken up by the motorcycle was overflowing with mismatched furniture. Under the bike, the renter's carpet was dotted with oil stains large and small.

The Baron gestured them to a couch sagging against the far wall and perched on a bar stool opposite them. A long bundle wrapped in a blanket leaned against the wall behind him.

"Your friend says you might need something fully automatic," the Baron said.

"I'm looking for click clack all right," Speedy said. "He told me you maybe got a Tommy gun."

The Baron grabbed the bundle and folded back one corner of the blanket. The end of a gun barrel peeked out.

Like a striptease, the Baron peeled back the blanket and let it drop to the floor, revealing the bluntly functional form of a Thompson submachine gun. She was the good kind, with the old-fashioned fat disk-drum magazine hanging down from the bottom like in a gangster movie.

Speedy pulled the wad of bills from his pocket and set it on the end-table. The Baron brought the Tommy gun over.

Speedy took the antique piece with reverent hands and laid her across his lap – she was heavier than he had expected. He detached the weighty drum magazine and inspected the gun.

The Tommy gun was filthy, and rusted in places, but the corrosion was only on the surface. It would take him hours with a toothbrush and about a gallon of cleaning solvent but he could get her gleaming again.

He squinted down the barrel. The lands and grooves were half worn away. The lack of rifling was no problem – Tommy guns were never known for accuracy and in the close quarters of the Mexicans' house he could not miss if he tried, even with this almost-a-musket.

Finally, the full automatic sear, the tiny piece of metal that determined if the Thompson was truly a machine gun. Speedy broke the gun down to reveal the firing mechanism and worked the safety selector control on the side while examining the complex mechanical innards. He swiveled the selector from 'Safe' to 'Auto,' watching to see how the top of the sear interacted with the other internal workings.

Sure enough, she was a full automatic; the Baron was not trying to sell him a 'machine gun' that could only fire one round at a time. Speedy leaned the gun next to him against the couch and grabbed the heavy drum magazine, held it up to get the Baron's attention.

"You got the magazine key?" Speedy asked.

The Baron lifted both hands, palms toward the ceiling. "For sale as is, for parts."

Speedy shrugged – he could wind up the magazine spring with a screwdriver or even a butter knife if he had to. He investigated the magazine well opening on top of the drum and his eyes widened: the drum magazine was loaded. That was why it weighed so much.

This just saved him case money. Fifty rounds of .45 ACP would have been a little spendy no matter how he picked it up, not to mention the paperwork he would have to lie on if forced to buy the ammo in a gun-shop.

If the Baron was stupid enough to sell a loaded weapon, that was his lookout. He was just lucky Speedy was an honest thief.

Speedy continued his inspection of the loaded magazine. The blunt copper-tipped .45 rounds lay next to each other like sleeping hornets, disappearing beneath the edge of the magazine's opening. He shook the drum, and the .45 rounds rattled inside.

He pushed with his thumb and the top round slid over with a metallic creak; he felt resistance as he pushed and the bullet returned when he released pressure. The magazine spring was good, then.

The Thompson was a clapped-old veteran but there was still life in her. All she needed was TLC from an expert. And Speedy was just the man for the job.

Speedy handed over the wad of bills and wrapped the Tommy gun in the blanket as the Baron counted his cash.

"All there," the Baron grunted in satisfaction. "This warrants a peace pipe."

He looked toward a doorway on Bob's end of the couch, and called out, "Kay."

A woman materialized in the room. She had frizzy blonde hair with black roots and wore tight elephant bell jeans and a tube top that left her pale muffin-top midriff bare. Even if she was dressed like a 15-year-old from a decade past, her makeup was not spackled on quite thick enough to conceal the deep lines carved into her face from too many years of hard living.

Kay held a pipe and a baggy of weed. She glanced once at Fat Bob before staring at Speedy. She did not look away from Speedy until the Baron hoarsely shouted, "Bring it here, woman."

Kay stared at Speedy one long moment more before obeying her old man.

The Baron finished tamping the bowl and offered first hit to Speedy. Speedy shook his head – the Baron wanted to be friends after business had been concluded, but Speedy wanted nothing more than to get out of this dump now that he had the Thompson. He had work to do.

Fat Bob leaned forward, reaching for the pipe. "I'll take that load," he rasped with a crooked leer, and the Baron handed over the pipe.

Speedy resigned himself to waiting while Bob copped his buzz – Speedy was not about to walk home carrying a machine gun.

Fat Bob hit the bowl, holding his lighter to the weed and sucking down a long hissing inhalation before passing it to Kay. She took the pipe and recommenced staring at Speedy as she inhaled, then let out a series of repressed coughs even as she tried to keep her hit in. Kay passed the pipe on to her old man, who toked it in turn.

The Baron sat on his stool, tattooed muscles rippling as his chest expanded to contain the smoke. His eyes were closed, and the smoke trickled dragon-like from his nostrils to frame his skull-face in a tracery cloud.

There came a furtive rustling from around the corner through the doorway Kay had appeared from. The Baron opened his own smoke-reddened eyes to look at something there out of Speedy's field of vision.

The Baron smiled. "C'mere, baby," he said, pot-smoke billowing from his lips to punctuate each word. "Come to Poppa."

A baby tottered into the room – a little girl two years old, with wispy copper-colored hair drawn up in two pigtails. She was naked except for one of those huge lunar-excursion-looking disposable diapers, the kind Speedy had seen mothers leave on their kids for a day or more without changing.

She walked unsteadily up to the Baron, grinning toothlessly with her eyes wide in excitement. She came to a halt in front of the Baron and beamed adoringly up at her daddy as he smiled back down at her.

The Baron took a deep drag from the pipe and pursed his lips as he leaned over to breathe a stream of smoke into his daughter's face. The little girl's eyes were half-closed and her toothless mouth gleamed wetly as she sucked the shotgun hit of smoke down, slobbering.

"God-DAM," Bob roared, rocketing to his feet.

The Baron started to reach behind his back and the blanket dropped to the floor as Speedy slammed the drum magazine into the Tommy gun and charged the action, chambering the first round of oh-so-many. Kay evaporated from the room with cockroach instinct and Speedy found himself between Bob and the Baron, hovering over the older man with the Tommy gun's barrel poised in his face.

"Oh no you don't," Speedy chided the Baron – or was he speaking to Fat Bob, bouncing up and down behind him?

The Baron's hand slowly came back into view as he leaned back as far away from the muzzle of the Tommy gun as he could get without toppling the stool over. His sweaty face was gray but blank as he displayed empty hands.

Something slapped against Speedy's leg and he looked down. The little girl was hitting Speedy, swatting at his pants leg with her pudgy little hand.

"Dada," she wailed. The sticky tears streamed down her fat red terrified face as she gulped air between sobs.

Speedy turned away and picked up the wool blanket. He kept his back to the Baron as he wrapped the Tommy gun.

Fat Bob still bobbed up and down in front of the Baron, though with less insistence. The baby plopped down on her diapered ass and commenced caterwauling.

"We're leaving now," Speedy said.

Speedy felt Kay's gaze burning into his back as he walked out. The baby's wails could still be heard as they reached the sidewalk. Behind them, somebody shut the front door and threw the bolt.

They reached the Valiant and Speedy put the bundled gun in the trunk, turned to face his friend.

"What kind of idiot sells a piece with rounds in it?" His eyes sought Fat Bob's, but Bob would not meet his gaze.

"You been away a hella long time, man." Bob looked back at the Baron's house. "He was the best I could do."

13: HAWK AMONG THE PIGEONS

Speedy, Little Willy, Fat Bob and Miya walked through the packed parking lot to the Alameda Penny Market entrance. The huge drive-in screen jutted up on the other side of the fence. They paid admission and entered the biggest thieves' market in the Bay Area.

It was an anything goes, hand on your wallet venue:

Hippies wandered the aisles selling macrobiotic sandwiches to professional fences, bikers went from stall to stall checking for stolen Harley parts and thumping vendors as necessary, prowling outlaws shoplifted from under-the-table antique dealers, and survivalists bought bunker goodies from undercover feds.

Willy peeled off to browse for first edition books. Speedy, Bob and Miya wandered the lanes. Bob bought Miya a pair of brand-new Rainbow Brite pajamas. Speedy purchased gun cleaning gear and three ski masks. As they came abreast the snack bar, Miya indicated thirst and Bob ducked inside to fetch drinks.

Speedy looked at Miya. "You may have your mom and your uncle fooled, but I got your number. You're quiet because you're a watcher. You're a kid that pays attention to the angles." He jerked his chin at a girl in the middle of a call at the snack bar payphone. "Who's she talking to?"

"How would I know?"

"Play along. Guess."

The girl was too far away to hear what she was saying. She looked unhappy and her mouth moved rapidly before she hung up and stormed away. Miya looked at Speedy. "Her boyfriend?"

"A safe bet. If it was a girlfriend, she wouldn't've rattled on like that before hanging up. It was a man friend, even her bottom boy."

"Go ask her."

"Let's not and say we did." Speedy flashed his eyes at a guy buying a ring from a vendor. "What's that guy thinking? What kind of mood is he in?"

"He looks happy. He's smiling. Do you think he's faking?"

"No. You can tell it's a real smile by the eyes. See how they crinkle at the corners?" He nodded at a man in a suit buying a cuppa at an espresso stand. "How much money does Richie Rich have on him? Where's he park his roll?"

"He's handing that lady money right now. He took it out of his pants pocket."

"You spotted his folding. But he'll have plastic too. It'll be in his wallet, in his breast pocket."

A salty looking kid leaned against the snack bar wall until a customer's approach roused him. Speedy nodded toward them. "Classic."

Miya watched them trade small objects, both green. "They think they're sneaky."

Speedy smiled. "You always watch their hands and you always watch for the exchange. It defines it."

Miya looked around the Penny Market, her face alight with excitement at all the people and activities, cuing in for the first time on the unseen food chain surrounding her.

Speedy said, "Here we are, hawks among the pigeons and none of them the wiser. They don't even see us when they look at us. They spend their days sleepwalking around and call it living. People like you and me, we own them. If we had time, I'd show you how to follow without them knowing you're there. You'd like that I bet."

Bob rolled up and handed them their drinks. Miya indicated she had to go to the bathroom. The men inspected the restroom and then stood guard.

Fat Bob said, "You know I love you Speedy. But for now I don't think you should be teaching Miya no more stuff like that. I know she needs to learn it eventually. But I don't want it crushed out of her just yet, okay? Humor me, let me pretend for a little bit longer."

Willy stood at the water's edge, his face vacant and forlorn. Behind him Speedy approached across a grassy field, past the Todd Shipyard Turbine Shop: a cyclopean pigeon-haunted multi-acre abandoned factory. Made of rotting antique brick, with hundreds of square feet worth of shattered windows gaping the walls. Beyond Speedy, Bob and Miya stood next to the Valiant in the Penny Market parking lot.

The Estuary was athrong with pleasure boats and working craft. Sail boats and cabin cruisers darted and flitted amongst their larger blue-collar brethren. To Willy's left was the Turning Basin, where tugs square-danced circular attendance upon incoming and outgoing cargo freighters.

Across the water at Port of Oakland, one of the big white container cranes was loading a ship. In front of Ninth Avenue Terminal, the floating island of barge cranes anchored together there bristled like a forest of masts and wheelhouses.

To their right at Coast Guard Island in the middle of the Estuary, a cutter was warping away from its mooring. Downtown, the Tribune Tower loomed above the other buildings. Mount Tamalpais was a distant backdrop, her silhouette obscured behind brownish smoke from wildfires elsewhere in California.

As Speedy neared, Willy said without turning "I could have done the time, Speedy. You didn't need to take the fall."

The tide was running and the water surged past from right to left at several miles per hour – even a powerful Olympic human swimmer would not be able to make headway against that current.

A cormorant paddled upstream against the flow, about twenty-five yards out. It dove and stayed under for an endless time before surfacing almost a hundred yards up current against the full-bore tide, with a fish wriggling in its beak.

The fish managed a few seconds of struggle before disappearing down the cormorant's snake-like throat and into its gullet. The cormorant dove again but did not surface within eyeshot.

Little Willy sighed. "Can you see how it all fits?"

Speedy said, "I could never see what you see when you look at things Willy. You should have been in college before you grew your first pubes."

Willy grimaced. "We both know that wasn't gonna happen. I used to see the interlinkings in front of me like a web I could touch, holding me in place. It was all part of a larger pattern I'd be able affect if I could just make that leap. I've lost it Speedy. I can't feel it."

Willy gave Speedy a haunted look. "The headaches are getting worse. I nod off into the fugues more often now, my brain hiccups and sputters even more than you remember. I sleep for days and the rats chew on me. I'm scared, Speedy. I want to go home."

Speedy said "Right now we must settle for TJ's pad, but not for long. I did my time up north, and I listened close to yard chatter. I seen and heard things on the way down too. There's land up in Humboldt, miles of it for cheap. How hard could it be, to buy property and become growers?"

"I don't know, Speedy. Tossing seeds on the ground and waiting for harvest might be a little harder than you think. But you're saying you're not just about the score this time? We got something waiting besides a spending spree and you roostering around like you always do after?"

Speedy laughed. "We won't have to move ever again and you can pile up as many books as you want. It'll be different, Willy. You'll see."

"Can I have a kitten?"

14: A GOOD CONVERSATIONALIST

Miranda opened the door wearing a low-cut red silk dress that clung to every curve, ending a bare inch below her crotch.

Speedy stood on the stoop. "Going out, I see. Bob here by any chance?"

Miranda snorted. "Is the Valiant anywhere around? You knew he wasn't before you ever knocked. If you're here you might as well come inside and take a load off."

Speedy sat at the table. Miranda reached down a couple of Flintstone jelly glasses and a screw-top jug of supermarket wine. She sat down across from him and they drank. Speedy had BamBam; she had Betty Rubble.

Miranda stood and strutted around the table, shoved the table out of the way, pulled up her skirt and straddled his lap. She had nothing on under the skirt and she ground against him, leaning forward to touch foreheads. She stared straight into his eyes, wearing her Mona Lisa smile.

She said, "You can stop me any old time."

She let the straps slide off her shoulders and her breasts rubbed against his shirt as she undid his zipper and positioned herself. She slid down and sat for a long moment, with the side of her head pressed against his chest.

She began to ride and he grabbed the underside of the chair with both hands. He sat still as she moved, slowly at first, then more quickly, breathing ever faster. He arched up against her and grabbed her as he lunged to his feet knocking over the chair, his hands squeezing her and pulling at her.

He was grunting and she yelped and moaned as he careened around the room knocking over furniture, her arms and legs entwined around him. He plopped her ass on the kitchen counter and plates smashed to the floor as they finished. After, they clinched for a while before separating. They rearranged their clothing.

She said, "Maybe I lay in bed too while you were Inside, thinking about might-have-beens. After our little spat, people wondered how itty bitty little me could make you cave like that. They were laughing for the first five minutes. When you went on the war path – all the doubters ate their words. No one was smiling any more. I was so proud of you daddy. But so what? We're not kids anymore."

The door opened and Bob and Miya entered. Miya and Speedy smiled at each other. Fat Bob eyed the overturned furniture and shattered crockery.

"Cat got your tongue, Bob?" Miranda asked. She smiled at Speedy. "He's just surprised I could be alone with a man who didn't have his pants all the way off."

Fat Bob donned a Jovian scowl. "Not in front of Miya, bitch."

Miya quietly said, "No, Uncle Robert." Bob subsided, chagrinned.

Speedy said "I think I'll leave before things start getting awkward."

Miranda grabbed Speedy as he left and whispered in his ear: "You're still mine."

Outside, Bob said, "What are you, Speedy, retarded? Look what it cost you the first time. Don't put your head back in the lion's mouth, brother. If you really need brown sugar, pick any Oakland sister but mine."

Speedy shrugged. "I know Miranda can bite; I'll have her chew marks on my ass forever. But she's just as good a conversationalist as I remember."

15: BOB FEELS THE JINX

The trio needed to case the Mexicans before the score, to scope out the house's patterns of movement and get an idea of how big a money train flowed through. For the past few days they had been doing shifts. Keeping their numbers different; either alone or by twos. Getting to West Oakland on the bus or by BART or being dropped off to watch on foot. Staking it out from various locations.

Little Willy was not allowed to pull any watches alone. Speedy and Bob reached that unspoken decision the first time they watched a passed-out junkie twitching in the gutter across from Alliance Metals, whilst behind him in Fitzgerald Park lighters bloomed and faded in dozens of spots as people hit their crack pipes in the shadows.

Speedy was lounging with Miranda this afternoon ('Do Not Disturb'). Willy and Fat Bob were lurking together in a '73 Vega station wagon. Little Willy had parked the car down the block from the drug house. A steady parade of mid-level people came and went at the house; people appearing several links up the drug trafficking food chain.

As the sun went down, faint with distance came the gunfire and yells accompanying the nightly slaughter over in Dogtown.

Fat Bob said. "I'm feeling safer and safer about using that for cover when we pull the score."

Bob watched Oso clump down the porch steps. "There he goes again, heading out for 40-ouncers and smokes like clockwork."

The neighborhood mom n' pop was right down the street from

Beau's. Instead of heading toward it, Oso walked in the opposite direction around the block. He reappeared at the far corner and entered the store.

Bob grunted. "This Oso cat is bright-eyed and bushy tailed. He's patrolling his perimeter."

Oso returned to the house with the day's supplies. He came out with Beau and Esteban. Beau clutched an aluminum valise as the trio walked to the Coupe De Ville. He carried it like it was heavy but still managed an arrogant dip to his walk.

Fat Bob sneered at Beau's flashy threads. "That one don't think much of himself, does he? 'Ooh, look at me. I'm a fancy pants.'"

Willy looked at him. "What, Bob? You think he's all that cuz he wipes his ass and shines his shoes?"

The Coupe de Ville surged from the curb. The Vega's engine made a loud, muscular sound as Willy followed them onto the Nasty Nimitz southbound. Willy had a challenging time keeping the car under control; the rear end wobbled at the slightest twitch of the wheel. The Vega behaved as if it wanted to run free and plow through all the vehicles ahead.

Fat Bob said, "This thing's hella front heavy. It's got something beefy swapped into it. Where'd you get it?"

"Ayefirmative on it having a 327. Also Offenhauser 360 manifold, Holly four-barrel carb, and a Ram-Flo air filter. As for provenance? Junkies always need money."

"You don't need a needle to be a junkie, Willy. We should put sandbags in the back to compensate for the crappy weight distribution though."

The Coupe de Ville parked in front of a motel off 66th, down the block from the San Antonio Village Projects. Little Willy drove past and hung a U-turn, a glass-pack crackling coming out the exhaust as he downshifted and parked across the street.

Bob looked around the hood. "We're the only pale faces in sight, Willy. Makes us blatant, don't you think?"

"What did you expect? We're in the Killing Fields of Deep East Oakland. They all figure we're either undercover cops, or cheapskates trolling for dark meat away from the official strolls.

Even then we got a few minutes."

Oso and Esteban flanked Beau as they walked past the motel's bar-covered windows and through the gate in the spike-topped iron fence surrounding the compound. They proceeded to an open door halfway down the motel's length. Two huge, skull-shaven Blacks flanked the doorway with forearms folded, both wearing shades.

Looking at the bullet-headed brothers, Bob had occasion to wonder if this was the same drug house Alden and Remy had gotten offed robbing; wondered if these two human book ends had been in on the kill. Feeling a jinx coming on, he swerved his thoughts back to safer channels.

Willy said, "I blew it, going crack head and all."

Bob grunted. "It wasn't about you, Willy. You started doing that garbage, it flashed me back to when we was kids. Remember that old junkie I used to slap around? He was my old man. He turned his back on us, and Miranda's panties dropped for the first short eyes mom staggered through the door with. I couldn't be around you, Willy. But welcome back to the land of the living."

The Mexicans filed out of the room; the two door guards still too chill to react. The three dealers walked back to their car, Beau now carrying a suitcase. There was a lot of something-or-other in it.

Little Willy pulled away from the curb to chug after the Coupe de Ville. "So you don't like drugs, but you always smoke and drink."

"That's different. You think we're gonna glom enough off them to swing it?"

Willy said "I think these boys are the mint. I think this is the one."

16: THE STARS ABOVE

The next night Speedy was taking his turn staking out the Mexicans, waiting for Fat Bob to show from the West Oakland BART Station and relieve him.

Like any other target neighborhood, the Bottoms had rhythms and routines that became apparent. The 'mad minute' of gunfire each sunset up in Dogtown was mundane with familiarity. The migration paths between the recycling centers at the Embarcadero and Alliance Metal – along which the neighborhood's homeless pushed their stolen shopping carts of cans and bottles – were marked by snowdrift trails of Styrofoam containers and food wrappers courtesy of 'free meal' handouts.

As for the target house itself, he lower-level dealers came and went from late afternoon to a little past sunset, stocking up for the wee hours. The honcho's runs to the apartment in the Grimy 90s took place every other day, an hour after sundown.

Speedy sat in the Valiant, alternately scheming and fantasizing about Miranda's tits. A black-and-white parked behind him, filling his rear-view mirror. It was Officer Louis behind the wheel. Officer Louis getting out and standing next to his OPD cruiser.

"This is District Four, is this even your assigned beat?" Speedy called out his window. "We're coming up on end of watch, Officer. You in the mood to do paperwork on OT?"

"I'm TAC 'Wild Car' these days, I rove where I please," Louis said, tossing his scarred head. "When your bosses hate you as much as mine do, you can do whatever you like and it doesn't stand out.

"Now exit the vehicle," Officer Louis commanded.

Speedy obeyed, conscious of the sawed-offer's weight dragging down the right side of his field jacket.

Officer Louis opened the back door to his roller. "Get in."

"Am I under arrest, Louis?" Speedy walked past the old police officer and started to enter, then leaned over toward him. "You going to guide my head, make sure I don't bump it over and over again against the door frame?"

"Do as you're told."

Speedy got into the cage and Louis closed the door, which made a *clunk* as it latched. Speedy sat on the hard backseat, which was polished smooth as silk from a million unwilling asses. He was not cuffed or micronized. He had a shotgun in his pocket he could pull out and aim at the back of Louis's head any time he wanted to.

He looked through the mesh of cage separating him from Louis as the fat old police officer slid behind the wheel. Louis's reflection stared back at him in the rear-view mirror. The keloid burn scars on the side of Louis's neck, face and head shone in the dimness of the car's interior.

"You like it back there, white boy?" Louis's reflected gaze left Speedy's in the rear view, and the police officer looked down the block toward the Mexicans.' "You like that house well enough. They ought to burn it down and sow the ground with salt."

His reflection looked at Speedy again. "You know why I never stepped on you? I liked when you took off other scumbags. Some fools are such wastes of space they oughta just dig a hole, get in it, and cover themselves up. Compost is the best they'll ever be and they're too stupid to even realize."

"But you did step on me Louis, that last time."

"I saw you at their trial," Louis said. "Was it funny to hear the judge declare tainted fruit, see the three of them walk free while my boy rotted in a hole in the ground? They sure were laughing on their way out the courtroom. You left town about that time if I recall."

"Yeah. Camping trip or something."

"That's you, the nature boy," Louis said with a bleak chuckle. "Those three, they dropped out of sight about the same time if memory serves."

"I forget. Maybe they left town too."

"Sure." Louis looked at the Mexicans' house again. "And you in jail a month later."

"Count the stars in the heavens." Louis pointed his forefinger straight up. "That's how many options you got in this world."

Speedy snorted. "Kind of difficult to see the stars through the roof of a cop car."

"I rest my case, Your Honor," Louis said. He sighed. "You would've been a good cop."

Speedy considered Louis's bloodshot eyes reflected in the mirror. The stale smell of unassimilated whiskey exuding past Louis's overworked liver.

Speedy said "I've seen what wearing the badge has done for you and yours."

"Get out of my car," Louis said, popping the latch on Speedy's door. "Next time I see you I frisk you for real, honky. And tell that putz Fat Bob he isn't near as sneaky as he thinks he is. I made him five minutes ago."

Speedy got out and Officer Louis pulled away. Fat Bob crept from the shadows to join Speedy.

"What was he on about?" Bob asked.

Speedy shrugged. "Just fishing, I think. But just in case, we must move soon."

"I don't know what you see in him," Bob said.

Speedy looked away, in the direction Louis had gone. "You may have noticed he didn't make the conversation optional."

Fat Bob grunted. "People see – they might talk."

Speedy glanced at him, eyes merry. "You think I'm a snitch, Bob? Payback's a bitch and snitches get stitches?"

Bob looked down. "He's pork, brother. And all pork can die screaming."

"I know who my friends are," Speedy said. "And I know what I owe Louis."

Louis was wrong about one thing, though. Here at street level, the brimstone illumination from the San Francisco Bay basin blazed so strong that it filled the night sky with impenetrable orange light smog.

Speedy could not see a solitary star from where he stood in the gutter.

Speedy and Miranda were finishing the deed. The Thompson leaned against the wall next to the bed. As Speedy rolled off Miranda, scars of all shapes and sizes were visible on his back. They laid side by side staring at the ceiling and gasping with hearts jackhammering.

Miranda said, "I don't let anyone touch me near as often as Bob seems to think anymore. You'd be surprised how many of the kinks just want to watch me do myself."

He said, "There's shit on my shoes, too. You and me, we're two of a kind. Oakland and me? I'll always keep it Bay and she'll always be my Oaktown. But she left me far behind while I was Inside."

Miranda stood naked in the bedroom door, smoking one of Speedy's cigarettes. She watches Speedy sitting equally naked at the table with the Thompson's parts arrayed on the blanket. He cleaned and oiled each piece with care. He reassembled her and stood, grasping her twin inline grips with tenderness.

He stood nude in the middle of the room, aiming the machine gun at imaginary enemies with glittering eyes. Miranda watched with eyes equally lambent as he swiveled on his feet, rear foot braced as he aimed the gun at all four corners of the room in turn.

17: DREAMS

Little Willy dreams of miles and miles of books. Of walking amongst corridors lined with stacked tomes and crowded shelves, deeper and deeper through a claustrophobic maze like an amusement park fun house of knowledge, or a haunted castle library. Each row of bound and printed heaven leads him closer to some final revelation that always seems just around the next corner.

As he does so often, this evening Fat Bob groans and writhes in his sleep on his sister's couch. Niece Miya stands next to him wearing the new Rainbow Brite pajamas her Uncle Robert bought her, watching his tears soak his pillow. Behind her, Miranda's muffled moans are audible through the closed bedroom door.

Officer Louis cannot sleep. His ratty-tatty old robe is open, exposing the burn scars extending from top of his head down to the waistline. He fingers the dusty awards and commendations lining the walls of his kitchen, holding a half empty bottle of brandy. He examines the black-framed photo of his son Philip and takes a healthy guzzle. He staggers over to his service pistol, picks it up and gives the cylinder a spin.

Ghost lies in bed next to Marla, who is on her side facing away. He awakes with a gasping intake of breath and an incredulous laugh, his hand clutching his neck. He is holding a big butcher knife and he drags the blunt spine of the blade across his throat, pressing hard. Ghost brandishes the knife.

He speaks to Marla: "I tried to spare Speedy but he can't be saved. With this knife I'll cut through everything that keeps him from me, all the way to his true face, his secret face. This time it'll be there, it won't be like with all the rest. The Others told me what part to eat for Speedy to make me real again. So it'll be all right, won't it?"

Ghost looks down at Marla as if awaiting an answer. He will have a long wait if he does expect a reply. He had finally gotten around to killing her the night before, when he brought home the knife to show it off.

Ghost lays on the edge of the bed, letting Marla have the wet spot as always.

Marla's at that cool, lovely stage of death between when he shut her up, and when decomposition will start becoming a problem. Ghost a little while before Marla starts to smell. He can still play around with her. However, it is only a matter of time before that stink begins, and Marla's downstairs neighbors notice their ceiling is growing a red stain.

Irrelevant. Ghost is increasingly excited about reaching the only possible decision regarding Speedy, and finally knowing their mission together. He longs to see Speedy again; he wants to talk to him so bad. Ghost looks forward to getting together with his worst friend, his best enemy in the world.

18: SUCKER PLAY

They were out of squares, so Speedy went out and picked up a pack around midnight. He stepped out of the liquor store, tamped down his cigarettes and tore off the cellophane, tugged out the first fresh smoke of the pack with his teeth. He lit his coffin nail and took that initial kick-start of a drag.

Down on the corner, outside a neighborhood bar, Speedy saw a man fumbling to get into a Beamer at the curb. This drunken Citizen was older, wearing a black silk tuxedo with loosened cravat and weaving on his feet, unable to get his key into the driver's side door lock and instead scratching up the paint job.

The Citizen turned to blink at Speedy, closing one eye and squinting.

"I need help, fella," the Citizen slurred, breathing out the fumes of a distillery.

"Give me the keys," Speedy said.

The Beamer handled like a dream; the interior smelled like money as well.

Speedy pulled up in front of the Citizen's house: a brown-trimmed English-Cottage-style on Gibbons in the Fernside District, one of Alameda's nicer neighborhoods. The porch light was off and the windows behind the manicured Rhododendrons were unlit.

Speedy helped the Citizen out of the Beamer, supported him to the front door, and wrestled him inside. No family dog charged from the dark; no wife or kid called out in sleep-dulled voices. No one was home but Speedy and his drunk.

In the master bedroom Speedy pulled back the spread on the king-size; laid down the now-passed-out Citizen, took off the man's shoes and covered him.

Speedy peeked in the closet, twitched open a dresser drawer: men's clothes only, no woman living here. Masculine toiletries only, in the master bath.

He moved through the house. One bedroom had two cots in it: kid's stuff, toys, and games. The beds had not been lain in for a while and dust covered the toys. In the kitchen, photos of two smiling boys were taped to the refrigerator, both in Peewee Football jerseys.

Speedy opened the fridge, snagged a beer. He sat on the couch in the living room with his beer in his crotch, looking around. The room was tastefully decorated, a woman's touch evident in all the stylistic selections.

Speedy finished his beer and put the empty bottle in the trash. He made sure the front door lock latched when he left.

It was a bit of a walk back to Miranda's but he had needed to stretch the legs. She squirmed around as he climbed into bed, but he rolled to lie facing away from her.

She asked drowsily, "What kind of sucker play did you just make?"

"Go back to sleep," Speedy said.

19: FALSE ENTHUSIASMS

Speedy and Fat Bob were pulling stakeout in Miranda's Vega. The Kid – the one with a passing family resemblance to the well-dressed Honcho – stood on the porch looking out into the night.

Fat Bob said, "So you and Willy are headed up north, after. I'm figuring Miranda's tagging along, and she'll never let Miya out of her clutches. But there's nothing stopping me from coming too. Right?"

Speedy snorted. "You needed to ask, brother?"

The sharp-dressed one – the Honcho – came out to join the Kid on the porch. The over-sized one in the cowboy hat – the one named Oso – accompanied the Honcho.

A girl walked up the porch steps toward the men, exuding false enthusiasm. The Honcho said something he considered amusing to the Kid, who responded with an apologetic look.

The Honcho placed his hands on the girl's hips and swiveled her around to precede him up the steps. The Kid and Oso followed as he herded the girl through the front door and inside, the Honcho still with that eternal strut to his walk even while repeatedly bumping his groin against the girl's ass as they walked.

"That one ain't nothing," Speedy said to Fat Bob, jerking his chin after the swaggering clothes horse.

Speedy switched his gaze to Oso's huge, receding back. "But that sidekick of his is deep dish trouble. He's got an ice cooled brain."

"I'll take him out like yesterday's trash," Fat Bob said.

After he went inside with Oso and Beau, Esteban headed to his room and commenced counting his rosary. Beau and Oso had their latest puta in the master bedroom; they were either tag-teaming or double-stuffing. Esteban could not be sure without going over and opening the door, but they often bragged about it so he just assumed.

Esteban heard the slapping of flesh against flesh. He heard the rhythmic cries of the girl, whether of pleasure, of pain, or a whore's simulation of either.

"Get your ass in here Steban, you little maricon," his brother yelled from the other room. Esteban kept counting his rosary beads.

When Beau and Oso were Beau came into Esteban's room without knocking and sat next to him on the bed. Beau studied the pictures of the Saints covering Esteban's wall.

"A stern looking bunch," Beau said. He gestured at the crucifix over Esteban's bed. "He seems very distracted by this whole 'crown of thorns, spikes through the hands and feet' thing, eh?"

Esteban continued mumbling his prayers and counting his beads.

Beau smiled. "The Man has enough problems of His own without your complaints, Steban."

Beau picked up the painted plaster Virgin Mary on Esteban's end table, holding her face to face. "This one, I can understand why so many would pray to her. She seems more likely to care when one is far from familia.

"You know I love you, hermanito," Beau said. "Give me a kiss."

Esteban obeyed, leaning over to plant a peck on his big brother's cheek.

"Bitch," Beau said. He laughed as Esteban flushed. "Padre Trejo is a liar and you are a fool," Beau said.

Esteban studied him, ready to admit his big brother was the Beast. And so long as Esteban belonged to his brother, he was part of the Beast as well.

"We're all going to hell," Beau said.

20: YESTERDAY'S TRASH

Little Willy sat in the easy chair reading a book. Fat Bob sat on the couch chugging a beer.

There was a 12-pack worth of empties on the coffee table, dead soldiers lying on their sides with labels peeled off. Label scraps were heaped in a funeral pyre in the ashtray next to them. Fat Bob lit the scraps and watched them burn as he finished his beer, belched, stood, and stretched.

He said, "Tell Speedy I went to take out the garbage."

After Bob left, a puzzled look crossed Willy's face. He opened the front door and looked around but Bob was long gone.

Fat Bob had to repress hilarity the whole time he was on the freeway. "The Groove Line" by Heatwave was on the radio.

"*Woo woo*," Bob keened in falsetto along with the chorus, and then succumbed to a laughing fit.

Once he hit West Oakland and the Bottoms, Fat Bob parked down the block from the drug house. Oso was crossing the street on his way to the liquor store.

Bob hurried after and stared through the window spanning the front of the store. Oso was paying for the day's beer.

Bob faded over into the alley to lurk. He waited for a while but the big Mexican did not walk by, so he peeked around the alley's corner to have another look at the storefront.

"You want something, puto?" Oso boomed from behind him. He must have double-timed around the block without Bob seeing.

Bob turned to face Oso. Oso wore a startled expression at just how freakishly bulky Fat Bob was despite his short stature. On

Bob's end, Oso was much bigger up close than from safe down the block

As if retreating, Bob backpedaled into the alley, trying to lead Oso out of sight of the drug house.

Oso followed smiling. "Wait until Beau has a talk with you."

"Up your ass with a splintery broomstick," Fat Bob snarled in his baritone rasp.

Bob lunged in with his quickest jab. Oso sidestepped and clothes-lined Bob across the throat, knocking him down to slam onto his back.

Bob scrambled to his feet to see Oso still standing in the alley entrance, nonchalant.

A blade snicked open in Oso's hand. It was one of those serrated little folders the length of a man's finger, the inconspicuous blade favored by someone who liked to get in close and do it right.

Bob kept his eyes on the cold steel in Oso's hand as the big Mexican closed in, waving his knife back and forth with mocking slowness. Bob faked high and then snapped a kick to the groin region that the big Mexican tried and failed to block– it landed solid and true, prompting Oso to hop up a little and roar in pain.

Bob danced back a step, then came in and slammed his most powerful punting kick into Oso's groin again, nailing the big man one more time. Oso grunted, hunched over.

Bob tried for one more nut shot to put the dip down for good. This time Oso rotated his hip enough to block the kick and stabbed Bob in the top of the foot. The blade poked out the sole of Bob's sneaker, and Bob yanked his foot free even as Oso ripped out the knife with a twist to spread the bones. The big Mexican giggled in a high-pitched little girl's titter and watched the blood spurt from the top of Bob's shoe as he backpedaled away step by hobbling step.

Oso closed in, extending the knife a little to try and put fear in Bob. Bob stepped in, slapped Oso's wrist with the heel of his hand, and the knife went flying. Bob tried to follow up with a palm strike to the temple, but Oso leaned back far enough that all Bob hit was the brim of his cowboy hat – the hat frisbeed away.

Fat Bob limped forward, slapping the heels of both hands at

Oso's upper body in a barrage of hooking palm strike blows. Oso covered up his head, but that was not Bob's target: his palm strikes were nailing the bigger man's arms and ribs, and the Mexican backed up with each blow, his arms flinching at every impact.

Bob's breath snarled through his clenched teeth in time with each strike. Spittle dripped from the corner of his mouth in a dense white foam, a whine came from his throat, and Oso was at the wrong end of a red tunnel.

Oso managed to lumber back out of range before Bob could finish numbing up his arms. Oso dangled his tingling arms and shook them.

Oso looked down at his fallen knife on the alley floor. He kept staring down at it until Bob could not help to look down too, to see what was so interesting about it.

With a howl Oso charged Bob with arms outstretched and grabbed him by the throat with both hands. The momentum of the heavier man's charge carried Bob back until he slammed into the alley's dead end. Something sticking out of the wall stabbed into the small of Bob's back as he hit – he felt something in his spine snap, and everything below his waist went numb.

Bob rammed both his thumbs into the Mexican's eye sockets, all the way to the second knuckles on both. Bob felt Oso's eyeballs burst like gristly grapes and laughed.

Oso howled again, a shrill note to his cry this time, and he slammed Bob into the wall again. Fat Bob heard more things breaking inside him, but he could not feel anything.

Bob slid down the wall to lie on his side as Oso staggered around in circles, his howls getting increasingly high-pitched. Both Oso's hands clutched where his eyes had been, and blood poured down his cheeks from the concealed sockets.

Oso careened out into the street. There was the blast of an air horn, and a Mack semi plowed into Oso and dragged him under, pulping him beneath the wheels and spitting out what was left of him in a rooster tail behind the truck as the driver brought his big rig to a stop. The truck's airbrakes hissed even as Oso's various remnants thumped and rolled separately on the street behind.

Shouldn't have come here, Bob thought even as he did his best to relish Oso's demise. *Messed up big time.*

"Miya," Fat Bob tried to say with his last breath, but it hurt too bad.

And then he died.

21: CHALK OUTLINES

When Speedy got to the Mexicans' neighborhood, the cops were leaving and the meat wagon was packing it up. Willy stayed behind the wheel. Fat Bob did not seem to be anywhere around, even though the Valiant was parked down the block.

Fat Bob was lying on the ground back in the liquor store alley by the dumpster. There was a chalk outline drawn around him, and his body was attended by homicide dicks. An over-sized cowboy hat was on the ground, peeping out from behind the dumpster.

Out in the street by the ambulance, there was another fresh chalk outline. There was another, older chalk outline beyond that one, on the far sidewalk. Turning in place and studying the surrounding blocks, Speedy saw more chalk outlines of varying ages and levels of sharpness in all directions, some scrubbed away and some not.

You could tell the relative ages of the chalk outlines by the amount of smog and airborne grit that settled on them as time went by, blurring them increasingly the older they got. The newer outlines were still crisp and clean, as fresh as the memories. The older outlines could barely be identified as human-shaped.

All these chalk silhouettes – mementoes from crime scenes past – were displayed around the liquor store and the neighborhood like a layered archeological exhibit of Oakland's history.

Gone forever: Speedy was free of Fat Bob at last.

Speedy's steps were slow and his feet like lead as he went to the Valiant and dug the spare ignition key from under the driver's seat. Little Willy followed him back to Alameda in the Vega.

22: BACK IN THE GROOVE

Little Willy sat on the sofa, staring into space.

Speedy said, "The gig's on for tonight, rain or shine."

Speedy left the room and Little Willy said to the air, "Foolish to ever leave me alone."

Speedy came out and noted Willy's absence. After a quick search he went into the kitchen and ripped the last cabinet off the wall, curb stomping it to kindling like the rest. "Fucking Willy! I wash my hands of your sorry ass."

Willy was on the AC Transit, heading down San Pablo. He went away, there on the back seat of the rattling, belching bus.

His eyes lit up and he gasped. His hand reached up as if to touch the street scene passing outside his window. He laughed as his face morphed into that of the man he was always meant to be.

"Splendid," he said. "Back in the groove. I'll never be alone. I'm part of it, too."

Tears misted his eyes as he exited the bus at 63rd. A little Black boy and his mother got off after him. As Willy stood grinning, they both stared at him.

Willy smiled at the boy. "Can't you see it? Don't ever let them make you forget."

The boy's mother quickly stepped away, jerking the boy's hand hard enough that his feet left the ground. He sailed horizontal for a second before touching down again, watching Willy the whole time.

Willy entered the basement and lit the candle. He walked over to his shit bucket and looked in. The dead kitten was still there, though bloated and maggoty, but the two rocks were gone.

Had he really been going to smoke them up? No, of course not. He was beyond that now.

"Welcome home, Willy," Ghost said behind him.

Little Willy reached for his .45 as he spun. Ghost had his arm wrapped around Willy's neck before Willy got even part-way turned around. Everything blurred into a slow-motion haze as Ghost lifted him off the floor and choked him unconscious.

When Little Willy came to, he was duct-taped to the barstool, seated in the middle of the circle of bloody rat footprints. Ghost stood in front of him holding a crack pipe, his hood down and his snaky dreadlocks framing his face.

"Shit gives the rock more flavor," Ghost said. He hit the pipe and held it a while, then blew a stream of smoke into Willy's face. "You always shared with me. Now you tell me how I can hang with Speedy again."

"We don't have to do this," Willy said. "I always liked you."

"You're just not good enough," Ghost said. "It's Speedy that deserves me."

"You'll never get him," Little Willy said as he looked straight ahead past Ghost. "He's leaving, he's gone. And he'll kill you when he finds you if you hurt me."

Ghost pulled a big kitchen knife from his belt and held it in front of Willy's face. Willy focused on his own reflection staring back at himself off that shiny blade.

23: HECK ON WHEELS

In the interests of saving gas Speedy and Miranda took the Valiant to TJ's. The pothead had not seen Willy. Speedy drove by the Estuary where he and Little Willy had watched the cormorant hunting before: still no dice.

They headed over into Oakland toward Willy's ex-squat. As Speedy was getting ready to turn off San Pablo onto Willy's block, the black rattle canned Econoline drove by in the opposite direction.

The Feathercut Girl was driving, her mouth opened in surprise as she looked over and saw Speedy making the corner; she mouthed a silent obscenity behind her closed window.

In his rear-view mirror Speedy saw the Oi-Boy with the Tam looking at him through the van's back windows with his mouth and eyes wide open as well. Bash leaned out from the shotgun window to stare back laughing, his nose heavily bandaged.

Speedy tromped the gas all the way to the floor even as Feathercut Girl smoked her tires and donut-ed into a sloppy U-turn, ignoring near collisions as she came after them. The Valiant accelerated sluggishly, the Econoline keeping up without effort.

Miranda turned and knelt in her seat, looking back at this van full of strangers howling after them. "Who are they?"

"The girl driving isn't very fond of me since I offed her brother," Speedy replied. "The guy in the shotgun seat, I stepped on his action. But in fairness, he'd ripped off Little Willy."

She swallowed. "At least you're still a people person."

Speedy continued down San Pablo with the van right on their ass. The Econoline kept trying to pass but Speedy swerved across the lanes to prevent them pulling up next to the Valiant.

Speedy blew through the stop sign at Ashby and turned left toward the Bay, almost clipping the center meridian as he merged into heavy traffic without slowing. Feathercut Girl was forced to stomp the van's brakes, balked by the clotted cars honking outrage over Speedy's driving.

Feathercut Girl took an opening several cars behind. Speedy continued under one of the railroad overpasses feeding Oakland Naval Shipyard.

Ashby transformed into an onramp curving north past the Mud Flat Sculptures to merge with the Eastshore. Rush hour was nearing its end but there was still plenty of traffic to dodge around in as they continued up I-80 past Richmond. The smell of meat cooked over an open fire wafted up from the Iron Triangle. The refineries infesting the hills around Point Molate. had tongues of flame shooting up into the air out their tops, even at a distance their hissing roar sounding like the pipes of a giant, diabolic calliope.

Speedy regularly checked his rear views in case Feathercut Girl tried coming up next to them again, but the van hung back. He said, "I'd let you out Miranda, but you're safer here."

"Okay. Whatever." Miranda was still watching the Econoline, not listening to him at all.

Speedy started to say something imperative. But instead he paused and his mouth slowly closed again as he focused on driving.

As they passed Hilltop Mall a motel stood off the freeway, above them off a frontage road on the El Sobrante side. There was a Denny's next door. An Alameda County Sheriff's and a California Highway Patrol car were parked side-by-side next to the eatery's entrance.

Speedy took the exit and the van followed them up the off-ramp. Speedy drove past the cop cars and stopped at the motel office.

He pawed a wad of bills out his pocket. "Get us a ground floor room away from the highway."

Miranda looked at him, then at the police cars. The police officers were inside the restaurant, eating together at the same table.

Miranda took the money and went into the office. She ran out and hopped back in the car.

"Room 108," she said.

Speedy backed the Valiant into their room's parking space. Feather Cut Girl hung by the lot entrance.

Speedy killed the engine and got out, holding the shotgun along his leg, and watched as the Econoline sped to the office and stopped. A stump of a skin with a face like a fistful of broken knuckles climbed out and swaggered into the office.

Speedy shut and bolted the door, tweaked open the blinds and watched. Miranda stood on tiptoe peering over his shoulder.

The van slid toward them like a cruising shark, then backed into a parking space nearer the street. Four passengers got out and stood in a huddle, staring over at the Valiant and Room 108. There was Feathercut Girl; Bash leaning on a cane with his nose heavily bandaged; the skin with the gnarly face; and the big Oi-Boy in his Tam hat. Feathercut Girl unlocked their room and the skinz filed inside.

Speedy stepped outside, only to dart back inside. Laughter spilled after him through the doorway, cut short as Speedy slammed the door and locked it.

"They're in Room 104," he said. "So, should we run across to those cops? I saw you looking."

Her eyes blazed. "Help from the pigs? Get real "

Speedy laughed. "That's my Miranda."

He sobered. "These cocksuckers think they can fuck me?"

The skin with the messed-up face was guarding the van, leaning against the hood smoking a cigarette. He appeared bored to Speedy – he did not even bother glancing over at their room more than once or twice a minute.

"They'll know I at least have the shotgun," Speedy said. "They don't know Fat Bob's dead so they're waiting to see if he's coming. They might even call for their own backup – but I wouldn't if I were them. They'll wait until the cops leave and then force us out somehow, gasoline bomb through the window maybe. Four guns against one."

Miranda held the phone to her ear, watching Speedy. He stood next to the door, peeking out through the blinds with his pocketknife open in one hand.

She dialed the motel office. "Could you connect me with Room 104 please?"

The phone rang. Speedy opened the door just enough to dart out bent over at the waist.

The phone picked up in Room 104.

"Hello?" Miranda said softly like she did not want anyone on her end to overhear.

More silence, then a man's voice. "You're the black bitch with Speedy. What you want?"

"Just checking to see if there's a way out of this for me. This is between you and the white boy, right?"

"Coolness," the man said. "Where is he now?"

"In the shower. How else do you think I could call you?"

"Yeah, cool. You let us in the room, and then you just walk away. Deal?"

The door opened and Speedy leaned in from the parking lot. He whispered, "Let's go."

Miranda dropped the phone and it thumped to the floor. She could hear the guy's voice still buzzing tinnily from the handset as they hurried out the door.

Speedy gunned the old Valiant as they headed out of their parking space and toward the street.

The gnarly faced skin snapped out of his sulk and pounded on the door to Room 104. The rest of the crew boiled forth; they were climbing into their van by the time the Valiant exited the parking lot.

Speedy floored the gas but headed away from the freeway onto a two-lane snake of a road, winding its way up through the foothills between townships.

Miranda was facing backwards again, kneeling in her seat. As she watched, the Econoline roared out of the parking lot and immediately began closing the gap between them.

She turned to face forward. "You said you took care of it."

"I cut their brake lines."

Miranda's head whirled to stare back at the oncoming Econoline.

The Valiant was into the first curve with a steep drop to their left. Speedy took it without braking, then straightened and barreled into the next curve.

Miranda watched the van as it overtook them until it was close enough, she could have spit out her window onto it.

Speedy took them into a tight hairpin at full speed, the Valiant's tires shrieking across the asphalt as the car drifted toward the sheer drop-off at the shoulder. Behind them the van roared into the hairpin just as fast.

The front of the Econoline started to swerve away from the drop as the Feathercut Girl realized she had no brakes – but the van was going too fast. The van rolled once, bounced into the air, and tumbled into space and down out of sight in a barrel roll.

The Valiant was coming out of the curve but their skidding drift had them creeping sideways toward the drop-off. Speedy had to stomp on the brakes to keep from going over the edge.

The Valiant lost traction on its worn tires and started a spin. Speedy's hands blurred on the wheel, fighting the rotating auto.

One second, they were skidding crazily toward the edge – then the tires regained traction and they rocketed away from the drop to slam into the hillside. Miranda heard Speedy's head crack against the door, felt and heard Speedy go *woof* as she flew out of her own bucket seat and thudded into the human cushion he provided.

She disentangled herself, unharmed. Speedy's eyes were closed and he was unmoving. When she hissed his name, he groaned and his eyes opened into gleaming slits.

She exited the car and studied the Valiant's front end, jammed into the hillside. The fender was bent but the body was largely intact. When she wrestled open the warped hood neither the block nor the radiator had been cracked.

Miranda sensed movement out the corner of her eye; about twenty-five yards back where the van had gone over the edge of the drop. She turned for a better look and saw someone or something pulling themselves up over the edge.

Miranda reached inside the car to fumble Speedy's shotgun from his jacket. Speedy called her name semi-coherently. She ignored him.

Turning back with the sawed-off heavy in her hand, she saw the driver – the Feathercut Girl. She swayed as she stared at Miranda and the car, her shirt front drenched in blood.

The Feathercut Girl started toward her, hopping along on one leg, wincing every time she applied weight to the shattered one dangling beneath her. She held a long-barreled .44 revolver. The gun was big as a cannon in the Girl's hand. The Feathercut Girl limped steadily closer.

Miranda stole a glance at Speedy: his eyes were open but he was gazing through the windshield at the embankment, unconcerned.

When Miranda looked back at the Girl, she was much closer. "Stop right now," Miranda said, aiming the stubby barrels of the sawed-off dead at her with both hands.

The Feathercut Girl did stop, swaying on her feet about ten feet away. Her right ear was half torn off. The Feathercut Girl mumbled through broken teeth, "You didn't win."

She began to lift her .44. Miranda let go with both barrels, the recoil wrenching her wrists up and almost twisting the butt from her hands, the kick making her stumble backwards a step.

She looked down and saw what a sawed-off shotgun does to a human body at point blank range. Miranda heard Speedy stirring in the car. He came to join her, blinking and swaying. They stood together looking down at what was left of the Feathercut Girl.

"My wrists hurt," Miranda said.

Speedy nodded. "That can happen with a sawed-off. You did good, girl. Let's check the others, and then we need to be away from here."

They walked to the curve and looked over the edge. The van lay belly up at the bottom of the gully about fifty feet down. They could hear the tick of cooling metal and a couple of minor rockslides tumbling down the slope. Nothing else.

They headed back to the car. Speedy dragged the Feathercut Girl's body to the drop-off and rolled her over the edge to join her friends.

24: COMMUNITY PROPERTY

Speedy and Miranda sat at her kitchen table hot boxing their respective smokes. Speedy held an ice pack to the swelling knot on his forehead.

He said, "You're not taking Bob near as hard as I thought you would."

"We all grieve in our own way."

He pursed his lips. "You and me, our past together is a little murky. With or without you in the picture Miya belongs to me now."

She said, "Just remember Miya's AFDC belongs to community property, not the general fund. You'll give me Bob's full share, fair and square. I'll be coming to Humboldt with you and Miya no matter what you planned before. You're not the only one tired of this town."

He said, "You just remember you're an accessory the instant we spend a solitary dime of the score."

Down in the basement at Willy's squat, Ghost heard a high-powered car chugging up to park in front of the house, and another car crunching gravel along the side driveway before stopping in the middle of the backyard. He put the duct tape gag back over Willy's mouth and blew out the candle.

Ghost removed the two-by-four bracing the door, and tugged the plywood open an inch or so. Behind him, Little Willy squirmed around a little, acting sneaky and testing the tape binding him to the stool. Peeping up the sunken steps from behind the plywood, he saw the Valiant's driver door open and Speedy step out.

Speedy looked around the backyard, and then peered down at the basement door. He thought of going down to see if Little Willy had been around, see if the little loser had come here to filch his rock cocaine out of that shit bucket.

Ghost looked back at him, yearning toward Speedy from the dark. Speedy took a step toward the basement but then looked back along the side driveway at something in the direction of the street and trotted out of Ghost's field of vision. Ghost heard an unseen car door slam and the car in front pulled away.

Ghost looked at the Valiant parked out on the lawn. Speedy would be coming back for that car, so Ghost did not need Willy now. It was time to wrap things up.

Ghost was not the only one who had seen Speedy visit to the house: Speedy had been on Officer Louis's mind increasingly. Louis was swinging around Speedy's old haunts, keeping an eye peeled for the ex-con to have another heart-to-heart and clear the air.

Officer Louis had just made the corner to do another drive-by on Willy's squat, when he saw Speedy climb into the Vega and leave. Louis drove past the house, eyeballing it with interest.

Down the side driveway in the backyard, Louis saw the rear bumper of the Valiant sticking out past the corner of the house. Officer Louis stopped to idle his cruiser in the street for a moment, considering that stashed car. He drove away.

25: FRIENDSHIP

Down in the basement, Ghost stood behind Little Willy and removed Willy's duct tape gag. Ghost held his cheek against Willy's, his chest pressed against Willy's back.

Ghost said, "Don't feel bad when you make noise. They all do. I won't think less of you."

Willy said, "Speedy's doubling back around on you. He'll kick in the door any second and then he'll kill you. Your only chance is to let me go."

"He's not yours anymore; he belongs to me."

Willy closed his eyes and scrunched his face away as Ghost loomed over him. When Willy opened his eyes, Ghost was smiling.

Ghost said, "A horror show filled with faces pretending to be as real as us and failing. I give you my gift."

Willy let himself look guilty. "He needs you more than I do."

Ghost said, "What is it saying now?"

"He's beginning to think he really should leave instead of just pretending."

Ghost whirled away to pace back and forth. He turned to Willy. "I forgive you for not being Speedy. Make up for it."

"Do I really have to suffer?"

"No. You are right, we were always friends, Willy. I like you for the rats."

"Speedy has had to act like he didn't need you this whole time. We both know why."

"Of course. He had to fool the Others."

"The others, of course. They're your problem. They can't know you and Speedy have something together. It would ruin everything for you."

Ghost paced back and forth again. "Go on and show me now, quickly."

"You're being too sneaky for your own good, don't you get it? Don't worry, Speedy's on your side. "

"I knew he was. I knew it knew it."

Little Willy said, "You doubt yourself sometimes, and you're right to. You must pause and re-examine every move you make with him. Take some time to rethink everything you do before you do it. Make sure Speedy knows you're there, don't creep up on him like you usually do. Talk with him first. The Others don't want you two communicating at all. Got it?"

"Got it."

Willy said, "Speedy will be so proud of you if you approach him openly. Stop and rethink everything, you can't afford to rush and make mistakes. That's the only way you'll beat the Others."

Ghost said, "It is good, to have a friend."

He stepped up to Willy with kindness in his hand.

26: THE DIVA ROCKS HER SOLO

Miranda swerved to the curb one house over from Beau's. It was a crap park job; she was at an angle with the butt end of the car sticking out into traffic a little. Behind them towards Dogtown, occasional pops of gunfire signified the nightly assault was beginning.

"I've got to pee," Miranda said.

"That's just the adrenaline," Speedy. He gave the Thompson a stroke before working the charging handle, chambering the first round of oh-so-many. He draped the blanket over the machine gun and got out of the car.

Miranda gestured at the three ski masks on the car floor. "Aren't you forgetting something?"

"Oh, no. I want these bastards to see my face."

She said, "If you play nice in there I might be waiting when you come out."

Speedy playfully swung the barrel of the Thompson her way, pretending he was going to aim it at her before pointing it back at the ground again.

The gunfire from Dogtown had become more frequent. Three dogs yanked a shrieking goat into view a couple blocks over. They were tearing it apart as a man came off a porch and shot one with a pistol. The other two lit into the man, each dragging at a leg so he slammed on his ass. The man's distant yell of dismay was audible even over the background gunfire. He blew one of the dog's brains out. When he aimed at the other his pistol either jammed or was empty. A terrified boy with a shovel ran down the same porch steps the man came from and commenced beating the dog to death as the man thrashed around trying to free his leg.

Speedy slouched up the porch steps. He put a drunken reel into his movements as he stumbled across the porch and pounded on the door.

"Michelle," he slurred, going for the exact same game as previously. "Michelle. This time I know you're in there, you bitch."

The door flew open to reveal the smaller guard from before, the one that put such effort into kicking Speedy off the porch. Speedy let the blanket slip to the ground and aimed in with the Thompson

There was something in the little guard's hand. He was raising it. Speedy sprayed a burst from the Thompson up into his face from point blank range.

The guard's head disintegrated in an air-flower of meat mist and bloody red chunks. Speedy got a mental freeze-frame of one of the man's eyeballs, intact in midair with an asteroid-belt halo of tumbling teeth and bone orbiting it.

The rounds stitched holes in the ancient lathe-and-plaster ceiling and white powder sifted down to frost them both. The ragged stump of his neck stained the plaster frosting red, making the guard resemble a headless snowman.

Speedy stepped over the body into the house, wiping plaster dust from his eyes with the back of his hand as he looked behind him. Miranda sat ashy faced at the steering wheel, but the neighborhood was still unaware, or pretending to be. There were no witnesses or cops in sight. Yet.

Speedy kicked the door shut behind him with a thrust of his heel and started into the front room. The other, bigger guard skidded sideways into the archway leading to the back room. He was racking a pump shotgun as he came into view.

Speedy let go with a burst from the Tommy gun, the right way: starting low and walking the rounds up into him. The bigger guard had not even come to a full halt, nor had a chance to raise his shotgun all the way before Speedy walked the Thompson's fire up into center mass. When Speedy let up on the trigger the guard's groin, abdomen and chest resembled a scooped-out bloody melon.

Speedy's ears were ringing from the Thompson's chattering song. The old girl was enjoying her vocal solo tonight. She was the diva brought out of retirement, and Speedy was only her newbie assistant lugging her around on stage for the aria. Speedy advanced across the front room with his finger ready on the trigger.

When he reached the archway, Beau and Esteban stood side by side next to a couple pieces of luggage, by a rolled back corner of carpet revealing an open floor safe. They both had pistols in their hands; both aimed at the floor.

Esteban aimed his pistol at Speedy.

"Goddammit, shoot him Esteban, you pussy," Beau said as Speedy made his tactical entrance into the room, the Thompson covering them both and ready to rock and roll. Tears poured down Beau's cheeks. "Don't let him do me, hermanito."

Esteban said to Speedy, "I'll be moving slow here. Just chill, eh?"

Esteban slowly lifted his pistol without pointing it anywhere near Speedy. Esteban aimed his gun at Beau, who was oblivious to this. Beau stared at Speedy with his pistol still pointed at the floor, right up until Esteban popped him in the side of the head.

Speedy's trigger finger cramped as he forced himself not to unload into Esteban at the sound of the gunshot. Beau crumpled to the floor and Esteban tossed his pistol next to his brother's corpse. Speedy lifted the butt of his Thompson from his shoulder and pointed the muzzle downward.

Esteban said, "You're here for my brother's money. It's all right here," Esteban said, gesturing with his chin at the two pieces of luggage.

Esteban stepped back to give him room and Speedy gravitated to the gym bag, holding the Thompson with one hand as he squatted and tugged the zipper open. He looked at all those bundles of bills; more money than he had ever seen in an eventful career of banditry. He picked up the heavy gym bag and looked at Beau's body, its head centered in a slowly spreading pool of blood.

"He was trying to go into Witness Protection," Esteban said, following Speedy's gaze. "He called the DEA after you killed Oso.

He lost his cojones."

"What makes you think I had anything to do with it?"

"I've seen you and your friends watching us for days."

Esteban looked through an open door into a bedroom. Speedy glanced in and saw all the religious paraphernalia; saw the Bible lying open on the neatly made bed.

"We're all going to hell," Esteban said. "That's what he says."

"Maybe so, maybe not," Speedy said. He gestured with the Thompson at the remaining piece of luggage, an aluminum briefcase presumably full of money. "All I know is, I'm by myself and in a hurry so I can only carry the one bag. There's nothing to stop you taking the rest for yourself and getting out of here same as me."

Esteban picked up the briefcase. The two men hurried through the front room together, each moving quickly as they could with a heavy load of cash dragging them down to one side.

They moved in slow motion past the bigger guard's remains. Drifts of stinking cordite smoke parted in front of them. The back wall, floor and ceiling of the room looked like a gang of psychotic children on Ritalin had attacked them with hammers and blow torches and then tossed a bucket of blood over their handiwork.

They stepped over the little guard's headless corpse and out the front door. Speedy set down his bag, picked up the wool blanket from where he had left it on the porch and draped it over his hot-barreled Thompson.

Esteban tossed his bag of loot into the Coupe de Ville and peeled out.

Miranda said, "Tell me you're not letting that joker scamper off with half my money."

"How's about you tromp it a little."

Miranda opened it up and blew past liquor stores and bars, past houses in various states of dismantlement and disrepair. The armies of homeless, encamped with shopping carts full of cans and bottles waiting for Alliance Metals to open, looked on bemused at the Vega's primal American big block roar.

They drove underneath the elevated Cypress Structure Freeway, the confined space echoing and amplifying the engine's howls. They drove past the lumberyards and crossed San Pablo Avenue, exiting West Oakland.

Behind them a roller swooped past toward Beau's house. On the other side of the Cypress a police chopper stooped in over the Bottoms with spotlight stabbing down. Miranda did not slow as they turned on the next side street, and the rear end whipped out like they were cornering at a much higher speed.

Miranda downshifted to the snap-crackle-pop of the exhaust, slid a playful glance at Speedy. "You don't drive this thing; you more aim it."

He said, "You probably want to slow down now."

She asked, "I wonder if you'd change expression if I reached over there and smacked your face as hard as I can?"

When they got to Willy's squat, they turned up the side driveway and into the backyard to park next to the Valiant. Speedy put the sawed-off in his jacket pocket and got out with the Thompson in his hands. He stretched, brandishing his machine gun overhead. Miranda exited the car and he turned to her with a smart aleck grin, opening his mouth to crack wise.

A police cruiser surged into the driveway, corking it. Officer Louis got out with service pistol in hand.

Louis's shoulder mike squawked and he reached up, turned it off. "You had to do it, didn't you?"

Speedy swiveled his body to face Louis, the Thompson aimed at the ground.

Louis's pistol was aimed at Speedy's belly. "You going to try and shoot with me with that thing?"

Speedy lowered the Thompson, unable to point her at Louis. The old cop plucked the submachine gun from Speedy's hands and dropped it behind him.

"You think you can ever stop running now?" Louis asked. "This isn't just 211 or even ADW. Forensics is all over the crime scene, and the Feds are involved too. A machine-gun assault, a houseful of DBs, a buttload of smoking hot money? No way can we finagle a walkaway for you this time."

Speedy spun to face the basement door, his right hand reaching for the sawed-off. Louis whirled toward the house too, dropping to one knee and raising his revolver to aim at the darkened basement stairs.

Louis was one fast fat man, but he was too late. A gunshot cracked out, and the muzzle flash from the doorway illuminated the backyard in a freeze frame.

A dark splotch appeared on the side of Louis's upper chest above the edge of his bullet proof vest. His pistol fell from his hand as he sagged to the lawn.

Speedy stood there with his hand not even dipped into his pocket yet, outgunned by someone quicker. Miranda stood frozen by the Vega. Ghost's upper body stuck up from the sunken stairs to Willy's basement, his hoodie snug on his head, holding a smoking .45.

"I knew you'd come back," Ghost said.

27: GREAT WHITE CHOMP

Ghost pointed the .45 at Miranda's head as he strode up the basement steps. Speedy raised both hands, fingers spread wide as he said, "I'm the one you got to talk to if you want the money. The pig and the bitch don't mean nothing."

Ghost hesitated for a moment with the muzzle of the .45 in Miranda's ashen face. He looked down at Louis and swiveled to aim at him for a few seconds.

Ghost tugged off his hoodie to uncover his nappy Medusa hair. He backed away from Louis and picked up the Tommy gun.

"You see, Speedy?" Ghost said. "I'm cooperating. Because we're on the same team."

Speedy caught a peripheral glimpse of Miranda to the side, squatting by Louis and holding his hand. She watched the two men interacting, but she whispered to the old cop.

Speedy said, "The money's not here. I'm the one you need to talk to if you want it. I'll take you right to it if you let these ones go. We can't make any more commotion; there's been enough noise already."

Ghost stuck the .45 in his waistband and pulled the knife, took one step closer so he loomed toward Speedy from his greater height.

Ghost said, "This is fated; neither of us can fight it. The Others can't stop us."

The muzzle of the Tommy gun was in Speedy's face. Speedy backed away from it until he butted against the Vega.

Ghost said, "I love you, Speedy." He aimed the Thompson's long barrel to the side as he stepped in with the knife.

Speedy dove sideways, sticking his hand in his field jacket pocket as he fell. Speedy was still in midair as he unloaded both barrels of the sawed-off up into Ghost's upper body without pulling the gun from his pocket.

Something hit the ground next to him as he impacted on his side: Ghost's hand, blown off at the wrist but still holding the knife. The killer's head bobbled atop what was left of his neck and blood spewed into the air – the double-ought blast had taken out enough meat, it looked like a Great White had chomped on his throat.

Ghost fired the Tommy gun up at heaven one-handed, holding back the trigger so the rest of the 50-round drum magazine emptied into the sky. His body crashed down next to Speedy and was still.

28: MECHANICAL DRAGONFLIES

As Speedy stood, the sawed-off started to tumble out the hole it had blasted through his field jacket. He clutched at the raggedy flower of green cloth where his pocket had been and held the sawed-off against himself.

Miranda knelt by Louis, holding the cellophane from her pack of smokes against his sucking chest wound. Her gaze roved Speedy's body. Louis' face was gray and sweaty, instead of the proud mahogany Speedy was accustomed to.

As if in a dream, Speedy walked past them down the stairs into the basement. Something called to him from the darkness that he could not refuse.

It was pitch black except for a sliver of moonlight spilling down the stairs and a little ways across the floor. Speedy fumbled around on the work bench until he found a candle but hesitated with the match in his hand.

He did not really need any light down here, did he? He could just turn and leave this basement; he did not have to know.

Speedy lit the match, touched it to the wick and turned around. In the candle's flicker he saw Little Willy duct-taped to the chair. There was a single stab wound up under Willy's jaw, and the front of Willy's shirt was soaked with blood; there was blood congealed in a puddle under the stool.

Speedy remembered his last night at home: Dad's trapped him in the kitchen, from which there is no escape route, and commences hitting Speedy repeatedly. Dad's fists crash into Speedy's chest, his face, and the side of his head – Dad is a strong man, his blows rock and stun the boy. Speedy cannot fight back, he is cornered and cannot get away. He accepts there is no way he can win. Dad's going to kill him this time, and Speedy surrenders in his heart, resigned to his own end.

Little Willy bursts into the room. He latches onto dad, but Willy has never been much of a fighter. Dad puts Little Willy in an arm bar and slams him face first into the wall. Dad smashes Willy's head against the wall repeatedly, each impact doing ever more damage to his brain. But Little Willy's crippling buys Speedy just enough time to come up on dad from behind with a steak knife...

Speedy needed to go to Willy now and embrace him. But he did not dare. This was a crime scene – Speedy could not bring himself to step in Willy's blood pooled on the floor, he could not risk touching Willy and leaving physical evidence for the Man.

Speedy dropped to his knees in lifetime-delayed self-loathing. How he despised this cold, selfish core which calculated only in terms of survival. He cried, in harsh, repressed sobs.

He heard Miranda mutter something strident out in the yard, and Louis' calm reply – the wounded police officer soothing Miranda. Speedy wiped at his face as he turned his back on Willy and went out the door.

"Move the roller out front," Speedy ordered Miranda as he came out of the basement. "Wipe whatever you touch when you're done. Then park the Vega across the street. Wipe it too. Be quick."

Miranda backed the roller down the driveway. As soon as she was out of sight Speedy transferred the money to the Valiant.

He knelt by Louis. Louis' hand was pressed to the cigarette cellophane, which was not making a good seal. Every breath made the plastic crackle as pink froth bubbled past its edges. His breathing was wet and tortured.

"Relax," Speedy said. "This is going to hurt."

He lifted Louis' hand away from the cellophane and grasped the base of Louis' index finger. He stuck the cop's own finger into the hole in his chest, Louis playing the little Dutch boy plugging the dike in his own gunshot wound.

"Oh, that smarts," Louis said, eyes closing as Speedy forced the finger as far into the hole, all the way to the third knuckle.

"Pipe down you old sissy. We both know you've been through worse than this."

Speedy rolled Louis onto his wounded side. The police officer coughed up a bubble of blood that burst to stain the front of his uniform shirt. Louis' mouth made an 'O' of surprise.

"You came by yourself," Speedy said to Louis. "No backup and no one knows you're here. Why didn't you call this in?"

Louis asked, "The scumbag who shot me - did he have a name or what?"

"He called himself 'Ghost,'" Speedy said, then squatted and picked up Louis' fallen service revolver. Speedy emptied the pistol into the back of the house.

"Louis," Speedy said, wiping the empty piece and handing it back. "Ghost and some other random guy robbed those Mexicans. You chased them from the scene to here. Ghost shot you, then his partner turned on him and blew him up with a sawed-off. You shot at Ghost's partner but don't figure you hit him and he ran off with the money. Say Ghost still has the forty-five he shot you with and they'll figure the partner has the other guns."

Speedy glanced over to make sure Miranda was still out of sight. He grabbed Louis' hand, said, "Willy's down in the basement. Ghost did him. Bob's gone too."

Louis did not pull his hand away. "You really killed them that time, Speedy? Did you kill those bastards that murdered my boy?"

"You always knew."

Louis rolled his head away, muttered something Speedy could not make out. His head rolled back to face the criminal. "You're finished now? This is the last?"

"I'm through," Speedy said.

"I never want to see you again." Louis fumbled at his shoulder radio. "I'm getting kind of lightheaded, Speedy," he said as he thumbed it back on. "If you're not planning on finishing me off, I've got to make the call."

Miranda ran across the street and hopped in the Valiant as Speedy backed it up into the street. Speedy took off at exactly five miles over the speed limit.

Miranda said, "Step on it. We need to be in the wind."

"Our only option is nonchalance."

As they drove east up 63rd, multiple clusters of cop cars barreled in from all directions, already on full alert from the drug house robbery. Although it was a fellow police officer on the line and most of them responded to the call's location, they did it by the book: units peeled off to interdict surrounding intersections in a multi-layered concentric circle, creating a net whose size was limited only by how many cops they could put in place.

A roller skidded to a halt in the middle of the intersection in front of the Valiant, blocking their path as the rookie driver mad dogged them.

"Look happy," Speedy ordered, putting an excited, entertained expression on his own face as Miranda obeyed.

He snuck a glance at her as they came up on the police officer, who fumbled at his holstered service piece as he exited his roller. Miranda's glassy-eyed grin was not cutting it; she appeared a little green around the gills. As they came abreast the young cop, he stood next to his open car door staring at them with pistol out (but not aiming it at them just yet, Speedy still had a millisecond or three).

"What's going on, officer?" Speedy asked in a gloating tone. Speedy was glad now that he had not run up and hugged Willy in the basement – this would be impossible to make fly if he were covered in blood.

The rookie cop looked at Speedy's expression, that of a powerless Citizen vampiric for suffering if it was inflicted on someone else. The rookie turned away from Speedy, already ramping up the career learning curve that would have him nod in understanding whenever a compatriot ate his gun.

"Move along, sir," he ordered, gesturing them the fuck away with a brusque horizontal chopping motion of his hand.

The rookie looked past them at all the strobing lights down the street where Louis had called from. Where the real action was, tending to a fallen brother instead of babysitting fools like Speedy and Miranda.

Speedy put a disgruntled expression on his face, the one any Citizen would wear when cheated of his vicarious thrills. They drove away. As they got on to the Macarthur Freeway, Speedy saw swarms of choppers hovering over where they had left Louis, mechanical dragonflies searching for prey that was already far, far away.

29: A BED COVERED IN MONEY

They got a motel room near the Oakland Airport, down the block from the Edgewater West Adult Resort XXX-rated motel. Miranda went straight to the bathroom but paused for a moment, her hand on the knob. "Bob said once, 'Speedy's the kind of monster that could run through hell with a sack of ice, still have enough for a sno-cone at the other end.' You still got it, daddy. For what it's worth."

She entered the bathroom and shut the door.

Speedy knelt next to the bed with the sawed-off and the Thompson within arm's reach. He spilled the gym bag of money out on the bedspread and commenced a fast count on the rubber-banded stacks of C-notes and 50s and 20s. He kept the TV tuned to KTVU Channel 2 while he counted, watching for any newsbreaks to see if they were hot or not.

The news flash came on: Dennis Richmond was the anchor, the distinguished looking brother with the moustache who had been reporting for Channel 2 since Speedy was a kid.

Dennis wore an expression of concern as he reported live from the crime scene. Willy's squat was behind him, lit by floodlights as cops swarmed all over it.

"A major story out of West Oakland tonight," Dennis said. "A gun battle at a suspected drug house leaves at least four dead. The assailants used a machine gun in the robbery."

Dennis continued droning on about the hit, and the getaway, and about Louis' heroic involvement. Dennis mentioned Little Willy's body being discovered, and that he was so far a John Doe.

The story ended without Speedy mentioned at all.

Miranda exited the bathroom naked and stood close to Speedy. "I always wanted to make it on a bed covered in money."

Speedy kissed her nipple and shucked his t-shirt. "We'll be doing it on top of 257,000 dollars. And some change."

"That may be enough."

30: THE AMERICAN WAY

It was midnight when Miranda took the Nimitz north toward East Shore. Speedy rode shotgun. Miya sat in back crying silently, as she had done intermittently since Speedy broke the news about Uncle Robert.

They started across the first cantilever of the Richmond-San Rafael Bridge. They were midway across toward the San Quentin side.

Speedy had the sawed-off and the Thompson in his lap. He rolled down his window and stared out into the night Bay's blackness, watching the bridge's gray hinges and trusses flash past. He tossed out the sawed-off and it tumbled away.

He started to heave the Tommy gun butt-first out the window but it was if the Thompson were glued to his hands – he could not drown this beautiful weapon. He lowered her back onto his lap.

Miranda said, "Don't throw it away if you love it. You might need it up north."

"Wait," Speedy said.

He chucked the Thompson out the window between two of the superstructure's beams. The machine gun flew out over the railing, the blanket clinging and fluttering behind like bat wings, as if the Thompson were an industrial Lucifer dive-bombing her way to Hell.

She was gone. The Thompson was going to embed herself in the mud at the bottom of the Bay. Speedy imagined boneless little sea creatures crawling over her, oblivious to her beauty and lethal power, and the Thompson rusting away in the end, leaving nothing behind but an iron-enriched section of ocean-bottom muck.

He said to Miya, "You shouldn't hang on to stuff you don't need. Especially if you can get in trouble just for having it. Understand? It's all right if you don't. You'll learn before I'm done schooling you."

Speedy snuck a peek past Miya through the rear windshield at the receding lights of the East Bay skyline; at Oakland's boulevards shining, her neon and sodium lights beaming up to drown the stars in that promise of riches and horror, splendor and despair. He tripped as he realized that he had raised from prison only the week before.

He turned to face forward. He asked, "Do you think it's possible to buy your way into being a Citizen?"

Miranda said, "Well, I think that's pretty much the American Way, ain't it?"

When Speedy looked back again a few minutes later, the East Bay was gone from his sight.

ABOUT THE AUTHOR:

Pearce Hansen was born in SF, came up in the East Bay, and currently resides in Humboldt. When Pearce was eight and attending his aunt's wedding, Jack Kerouac snuck him champagne.

Photo: Sheldon Sabbatini

Made in United States
Orlando, FL
18 July 2025

63074134R10074